'Flann O'Brien' was one of the two pseudonyms made illustrious by Brian O'Nolan. He wrote four novels in English – *The Third Policeman*, *The Dalkey Archive*, *The Hard Life* (all published in Picador) and *At Swim-Two-Birds*, as well as the famous work in Irish, *An Béal Bocht*, now translated as *The Poor Mouth*.

Under the name 'Miles na Gopaleen', he wrote a famous column in the *Irish Times* – selections from which are also published in Picador as *The Best of Myles*.

He was born in County Tyrone in 1911 and died in Dublin in 1966. His reputation is still growing.

THE POOR MOUTH
(An Béal Bocht)

A bad story about the hard life

Edited by

MYLES na GOPALEEN
(FLANN O'BRIEN)

Translated by
PATRICK C. POWER

and Illustrated by
RALPH STEADman

'if a stone be cast, there is no
foreknowledge of where it may land' p.■

PICADOR, Pan Books

Also by Flann O'Brien in Picador

The Dalkey Archive
The Hard Life
The Third Policeman
The Best of Myles

First published in Great Britain 1973 by
Hart-Davis, MacGibbon Ltd
This Picador edition published 1975 by
Pan Books Ltd, Cavaye Place, London SW10 9PG
7th printing 1983
An Beal Bocht first published 1941 by The Dolmen Press Ltd
Copyright © Evelyn O'Nolan
Translation © Hart-Davis, MacGibbon Ltd 1973
ISBN 0 330 24584 8
Printed in Great Britain by
Fletcher & Son Ltd, Norwich

Translator's Preface

THIS CELEBRATED satirical work, *An Béal Bocht*, first published in 1941, is here translated for the first time under the title of *The Poor Mouth*. In Gaelic and in Anglo-Irish dialect, 'putting on the poor mouth' means making a pretence of being poor or in bad circumstances in order to gain advantage for oneself from creditors or prospective creditors. It may also mean simply 'grumbling' according to the lexicographer Dr Patrick Dinneen, a scholar who received scant respect from Myles na Gopaleen.

The author, Brian O'Nolan, who writes under his *nom de plume*, Myles na Gopaleen, was an accomplished Gaelic scholar and handles Gaelic in this work in a masterly but also in a rather idiosyncratic manner which makes translation at times a rather exacting task.

The third edition, which contains many interpolations and emendations, is the text translated here. Wherever this particular edition presented difficulties or ambiguities, the earlier editions have been consulted. In this text the author included some humorous 'translations' of single words which he added to the ends of the pages as footnotes. They occur only in the first chapter of the third edition and have been included here in notes at the back of the book.

In *The Poor Mouth* Myles comments mercilessly on Irish life and not only on the Gaeltacht. Words such as 'hard times', 'poverty', 'drunkenness', 'spirits' and 'potatoes' recur in the text with almost monotonous regularity. The atmosphere reeks of the rain and the downpour and with relentless insistence he speaks of people who are 'facing for eternity' and the like. The key-words in this work are surely 'downpour', 'eternity' and 'potatoes' set against a background of squalor and poverty.

The principal difficulty attending the translation of this work has been due to Myles's parodying the style of certain Gaelic authors such as Máire (Séamas Ó Grianna) from the Rosses in County Donegal and Tomás Ó Criomhthainn from the Great Blasket Island in County Kerry. This daunting task must always face the translator who wishes to reproduce in another language the subtle nuances and flavour of the original.

For too long *An Béal Bocht* has been inaccessible to those who were ignorant of Gaelic or whose knowledge of the old language of Ireland was inadequate for a proper understanding of Myles's satirical work. It is time that this book, which should have acted as a cauterisation of the wounds inflicted on Gaelic Ireland by its official friends, might do its work in the second official language of Ireland. That it may do so, is the translator's wish and hope.

Patrick C. Power M.A., Ph.D.

Preface to the First Edition

I BELIEVE THAT this is the first book ever published on the subject of Corkadoragha. It is timely and opportune, I think. Of great advantage both to the language itself and to those studying it is that a little report on the people who inhabit that remote Gaeltacht should be available after their times and also that some little account of the learned smooth Gaelic which they used should be obtainable.

This document is exactly as I received it from the author's hand except that much of the original matter has been omitted due to pressure of space and to the fact that improper subjects were included in it. Still, material will be available ten-fold if there is demand from the public for the present volume.

It is understandable that anything mentioned here concerns only Corkadoragha and it is not to be understood that any reference is intended to the Gaeltacht areas in general; Corkadoragha is a distinctive place and the people who live there are without compare.

It is a cause of jubilation that the author, Bonaparte O'Coonassa, is still alive today, safe in jail and free from the miseries of life.

The Editor
The Day of Want, 1941

FORE

CHINA

← Un

M.O

ABROAD

M.O.

M.O

1
2
3

SEA of TROUBLES

TORY
ARAN
BLASKET

CORKADOR

P. de P

Long-horned Cows
Sea-divided Gaels
Poteen deposits
Green hills
① New Lark
② Boston
③ Springfield. Mass.
M.O. Money Order Office
G.B.S. George Bernard Shaw
--- Pratie Hokers' Routes

FOREIG

Foreword

IT IS SAD to relate that neither praise nor commendation is deserved by Gaelic folk—those of them who are moneyed gentle-folk or great bucks (in their own estimation)—because they have allowed a fascicle such as *The Poor Mouth* to remain out of print for many years; without young or old having an opportunity to see it, nor having any chance of milking wisdom, shrewdness and strength from the deeds of the unusual community that lives west in Corkadoragha—the seed of the strong and the choicest of paupers.

They live there to this day, but they are not increasing in numbers and the sweet Gaelic dialect, which is oftener in their mouths than a scrap of food, is not developing but rather declining like rust. Apart from this fact, emigration is thinning out the remote areas, the young folk are setting their faces towards Siberia in the hope of better weather and relief from the cold and tempest which is natural to them.

I recommend that this book be in every habitation and mansion where love for our country's traditions lives at this hour when, as Standish Hayes O'Grady says 'the day is drawing to a close and the sweet wee maternal tongue has almost ebbed'.

The Editor
The Day of Doom, 1964

Chapter 1

I AM NOTING down the matters which are in this document because the next life is approaching me swiftly—far from us be the evil thing and may the bad spirit not regard me as a brother!—and also because our likes will never be there again. It is right and fitting that some testimony of the diversions[1] and adventures[2] of our times should be provided for those who succeed us because our types will never be there again nor any other life in Ireland comparable to ours who exists no longer.

O'Coonassa is my surname in Gaelic, my first name is Bonaparte and Ireland is my little native land. I cannot truly remember either the day I was born or the first six months I spent here in the world. Doubtless, however, I was alive at that time although I have no memory of it, because I should not exist now if I were not there then and to the human being, as well as to every other living creature, sense comes gradually.

♣ *The night before I was born, it happened that my father and Martin O'Bannassa were sitting on top of the hen-house, gazing at the sky to judge the weather and also chatting honestly and quietly about the difficulties of life.*

— Well, now, Martin, said my father, the wind is from the north and there's a forbidding look about the White Bens: before the morning there'll be rain and we'll get a dirty tempestuous night of it that will knock a shake out of us even if we're in the very bed. And look here! Martin, isn't it the bad sign that the ducks are in the nettles?

The night before I was born, it happened that my father and Martin O'Bannassa were sitting on top of the hen-house, gazing at the sky to judge the weather and also chatting honestly and quietly about the difficulties of life.

- Well, now, Martin, said my father, the wind is from the north and there's a forbidding look about the White Bens; before the morning there'll be rain and we'll get a dirty tempestuous night of it that will knock a shake out of us even if we're in the very bed. And look here! Martin, isn't it the bad sign that the ducks are in the nettles? Horror and misfortune will come on the world tonight; the evil thing and sea-cat will be a-foot in the darkness and, if 'tis true for me, no good destiny is ever in store for either of us again.

- Well, indeed, Michelangelo, said Martin O'Bannassa, 'tis no little thing you've said there now and if you're right, you've told nary a lie but the truth itself.

I was born in the middle of the night in the end of the house.[3] My father never expected me because he was a quiet fellow and did not understand very accurately the ways of life. My little bald skull so astounded him that he almost departed from this life the moment I entered it and, indeed, it was a misfortune and harmful thing for him that he did not, because after that night he never had anything but misery and was destroyed and rent by the world and bereft of his health as long as he lived. The people said that my mother was not expecting me either and it is a fact that the whisper went around that I was not born of my mother at all but of another woman. All that, nevertheless, is only the neighbours' talk and cannot be checked now because the neighbours are all dead and their likes will not be there again. I never laid eyes on my father until I was grown up but that is another story and I shall mention it at another time in this document.

I was born in the West of Ireland on that awful winter's

night—may we all be healthy and safe!—in the place called Corkadoragha and in the townland named Lisnabrawshkeen. I was very young at the time I was born and had not aged even a single day; for half a year I did not perceive anything about me and did not know one person from the other. Wisdom and understanding, nevertheless, come steadily, solidly and stealthily into the mind of every human being and I spent that year on the broad of my back, my eyes darting here and there at my environment. I noticed my mother in the house before me, a decent, hefty, big-boned woman; a silent, cross, big-breasted woman. She seldom spoke to me and often struck me when I screamed in the end of the house. The beating was of little use in stopping the tumult because the second tumult was worse than the first one and, if I received a further beating, the third tumult was worse than the second one. However, my mother was sensible, level-headed and well-fed; her like will not be there again. She spent her life cleaning out the house, sweeping cow-dung and pig-dung from in front of the door, churning butter and milking cows, weaving and carding wool and working the spinning-wheel, praying, cursing and setting big fires to boil a houseful of potatoes to stave off the day of famine.

There was another person in the house in front of me—an old crooked, stooped fellow with a stick, half of whose face and all of whose chest were invisible because there was a wild, wool-grey beard blocking the view. The hairless part of his face was brown, tough and wrinkled like leather and two sharp shrewd eyes looked out from it at the world with a needle's sharpness. I never heard him called anything but the Old-Grey-Fellow. He lived in our house and very often my mother and he were not of the same mind and, bedad, it was an incredible thing the amount of potatoes he consumed, the volume of speech which issued from him and what little work he performed around the house. At first in my youth I thought he was my father. I remember sitting in his company one night, both of us gazing peacefully into the great red mass of the fire where my mother had placed a pot of potatoes as big as a barrel a-boiling for the pigs—she herself was quiet in the end of the house. It happened that the heat of the fire was roasting me but I was not able to walk at that time and had no means of escape from the heat on my own. The Old-Grey-Fellow cocked an eye at me and announced:

- 'Tis hot, son!

- There's an awful lot of heat in that fire truly, I replied, but look, sir, you called me son for the first time. It may be that you're my father and that I'm your child, God bless and save us and far from us be the evil thing!

- 'Tisn't true for you, Bonaparte, said he, for I'm your grandfather. Your father is far from home at the present but his name and surname in his present habitation are Michelangelo O'Coonassa.

- And where is he?

- He's in the jug! said the Old-Grey-Fellow.

At that time I was only about in the tenth month of my life but when I had the opportunity I looked into the jug. There was nothing in it but sour milk and it was a long time until I understood the Old-Grey-Fellow's remark, but that is another story and I shall mention it in another place in this document.

There is another day of my youth which is clear in my memory and eminently describable. I was sitting on the floor of the house, still unable to walk or even stand and watching my mother sweeping the house and settling the hearth neatly with the tongs. The Old-Grey-Fellow came in from the field and stood looking at her until she had finished the work.

- Woman, said he, it is a harmful, untimely work that you're at there and you may be sure that neither good nor fine instruction will come of it for the fellow who's there on his backside on the floor of our house.

- Any word and nearly every sound out of you are sweet to me, said she, but truly I don't understand what you're saying.

- Well, said the Old-Fellow, when I was a raw youngster growing up, I was (as is clear to any reader of the good Gaelic books) a child among the ashes.[4] You have thrown all the ashes of the house back into the fire or swept them out in the yard and not a bit left for the poor child on the floor—he pointed a finger towards me—to let him into. It's an un-natural and unregulated training and rearing he'll have without any experience of the ashes. Therefore, woman, it's disgraceful for you not to leave the hob full of dirt and ashes just as the fire leaves it.

- Very well, said my mother, 'tis true for you although you seldom talk a bit of sense and I'll be glad to put back all I swept from the hob.

And she did so. She took a bucket full of muck, mud and ashes and hen's droppings from the roadside and spread it around the hearth gladly in front of me. When everything was arranged, I moved over near the fire and for five hours I became a child in the ashes—a raw youngster rising up according to the old Gaelic tradition. Later at midnight I was taken and put into bed but the foul stench of the fireplace stayed with me for a week; it was a stale, putrid smell and I do not think that the like will ever be there again.

We lived in a small, lime-white, unhealthy house, situated in a corner of the glen on the right-hand side as you go eastwards along the road. Doubtless, neither my father nor any of his people before him built the house and placed it there; it is not known whether it was god, demon or person who first raised the half-rotten, rough walls. If there were a hundred corners in all that glen, there was a small lime-white cabin nestling in each one and no one knows who built any

♣ She took a bucket full of muck, mud and ashes and hen's droppings from the roadside, and spread it around the hearth gladly in front of me. When everything was arranged, I moved over near the fire and for five hours I became a child in the ashes—a raw youngster rising up according to the old Gaelic tradition. Later at midnight I was taken and put into bed but the foul stench of the fireplace stayed with me for a week; it was a stale, putrid smell and I do not think that the like will ever be there again.

of them either. It has always been the destiny of the true Gaels (if the books be credible) to live in a small, lime-white house in the corner of the glen as you go eastwards along the road and that must be the explanation[5] that when I reached this life there was no good habitation for me but the reverse in all truth. As well as the poverty of the house in itself, it clung to a lump of rock on the perilous shoulder of the glen (although there was a fine site available lower down) and if you went out the door without due care as to where you stepped, you could be in mortal danger immediately because of the steep gradient.

Our house was undivided, wisps of rushes above us on the roof and rushes also as bedding in the end of the house. At sundown rushes were spread over the whole floor and the household lay to rest on them. Yonder a bed with pigs upon it; here a bed with people; a bed there with an aged slim cow stretched out asleep on her flank and a gale of breath issuing from her capable of raising a tempest in the centre of the house; hens and chickens asleep in the shelter of her belly; another bed near the fire with me on it.

Yes! people were in bad circumstances when I was young and he who had stock and cattle possessed little room at night in his own house. Alas! it was always thus. I often heard the Old-Grey-Fellow speak of the hardship and misery of life in former times.

- There was a time, said he, when I had two cows, a cart-horse, a race-horse, sheep, pigs and other lesser animals.[6] The house was narrow and, upon me soul, 'twas a tight troublesome situation we were in when the night came. My grandfather slept with the cows and I myself slept with the horse, Charlie, a quiet, gentle animal. The sheep used often start fighting and many times I went without a wink of sleep from the bleating and the roaring they used have. One night my grandfather was hurt and wounded but we didn't know

♣ *The sheep used often start fighting and many times I went without a wink of sleep from the bleating and the roaring they used have.*

whether 'twas the sheep or the cows that were the cause of it or whether my grandmother herself started the quarrel. But another night a gentleman arrived, a school-inspector that went astray in the bog-mist and happened to come on the mouth of the glen. Looking for help and lodging he was, maybe, and when he saw what was to be seen in the low light of the fire, he let a long roar of amazement out of him and stood there on the threshold staring in. Says he: Isn't it a shameful, improper and very bad thing for ye to be stretched out with the brute beasts, all of ye stuck together in the one bed? And isn't it a shameful, bad and improper state that ye're in here tonight? 'Tis true for you, I replied to the gentleman, but sure we can't help the bad state you've mentioned. The weather is bitter and everyone of us must be inside from it, whether he has two legs or four under him. If that's the way it is, says the gentleman, wouldn't it be easy for you to put up a little hut at the side of the yard and it a bit out from the house? Sure and 'twould be easy, says I. I was full of wonder at all he said because I never thought of the like nor of any other plan that would be handy to improve the bad state we were in—all of us stuck together in the end of the house. The next day I gathered the neighbours and explained exactly to them the gentleman's advice. They praised that advice and within a week we had put up a fine hut adjacent to my house. But alas! things are not what they seem to be! When I, my grandmother and two of my brothers had spent two nights in the hut, we were so cold and drenched wet that it is a wonder we did not die straight away and we couldn't get any relief until we went back to the house and were comfortable again among the cattle. We've been that way ever since, just like every poor bit of a Gael in this side of the country.

The Old-Grey-Fellow often provided accounts such as this of the old times and from him I received much of the sense and wisdom which is now mine. However, concerning the house where I was born, there was a fine view from it. It had two windows with a door between them. Looking out from the right-hand window, there below was the bare hungry countryside of the Rosses and Gweedore; Bloody Foreland yonder and Tory Island far away out, swimming like a great ship where the sky dips into the sea. Looking out of the door, you could see the West of County Galway with a good portion of the rocks of Connemara, Aranmore in the ocean out from you with the small bright houses of Kilronan, clear and visible, if your eyesight were good and the Summer had come. From the window on the left you could see the Great Blasket, bare and forbidding as a horrible other-worldly eel, lying languidly on the wave-tops; over yonder was Dingle with its houses close together. It has always been said that there is no view from any house in Ireland comparable to this and it must be admitted that this statement is true. I have never heard it said that there was any house as well situated as this on the face of the earth. And so this house was delightful and I do not think that its like will ever be there again.[7] At any rate, I was born there and truly this cannot be stated concerning any other house, whether that fact be praise or blame!

Chapter 2

A bad smell in our house ♣ the pigs ♣ the coming of Ambrose

♣ the hard life ♣ my mother in danger of death ♣ Martin's

---

plan ♣ we are saved and are safe ♣ the death of Ambrose

I N MY YOUTH we always had a bad smell in our house. Sometimes it was so bad that I asked my mother to send me to school, even though I could not walk correctly. Passers-by neither stopped nor even walked when in the vicinity of our house but raced past the door and never ceased until they were half a mile from the bad smell. There was another house two hundred yards down the road from us and one day when our smell was extremely bad the folks there cleared out, went to America and never returned. It was stated that they told people in that place that Ireland was a fine country but that the air was too strong there. Alas! there was never any air in our house.

A member of our household was guilty of this stench. Ambrose was his name. The Old-Fellow was very attached to him. Ambrose was Sarah's son. Sarah was a sow which we possessed and when progeny was bestowed on her, it was bestowed plentifully. In spite of her numerous breasts, there was none for Ambrose when the piglets were sucking their nourishment from her. Ambrose was shy and when hunger struck the piglets (it strikes their likes suddenly and all at the same moment) he was left at the end without a breast. When the Old-Fellow realised that this little piglet was becoming feeble and losing his vigour, he brought him into the house, settled a bed of rushes for him by the fireside and fed him from time to time with cow's milk out of an old bottle. Ambrose recovered without delay, grew strongly and became fine and fat. But alas! God has permitted every creature to possess its own smell and the pig's inherited aroma is not pleasant. When Ambrose was little, he had a little smell. When his size increased, his smell grew accordingly. When he was big, the smell was likewise big. At first, the situation was not too bad for us throughout the day, because we left all the windows open, the door unshut and great gales of wind swept through the house. But when darkness fell and Sarah came in with the piglets to sleep, that indeed was the situation which defies both oral and written description. Often in the middle of the night it seemed to us that we could never see the morning alive. My mother and the Old-Fellow often arose and went outside to walk ten miles in the rain trying to escape from the stench. After about a month of Ambrose in our house, the horse, Charlie, refused to come in at night and was found every morning drenched and wet (there was never a night without a downpour upon us). But he was, nevertheless, in good humour despite all he had suffered from the inclemency of the weather. Indeed, it was I who bore the hardship without a doubt because I could not walk nor find any means of self-locomotion.

Matters continued thus for a little while. Ambrose was swelling rapidly and the Old-Grey-Fellow said that shortly he would be strong enough to be out in the air with the other pigs. He was the Old-Fellow's pet and that is why my mother could not drive out the unfragrant pig from the house by cudgelling, although her health was failing due to the putrid stench.

We noticed suddenly that Ambrose, all in one night it seemed, had increased to a fearful size. He was as tall as his mother but much wider. His belly reached the ground and his flanks were so swollen that they would frighten you. One day the Old-Grey-Fellow was putting down a large pot of potatoes for the pig's dinner when he noticed that all was neither good nor natural.

- Upon me soul! said he, this one here is about to burst!

When we scrutinised Ambrose sharply, it was evident that the poor creature was almost completely cylindrical. I do not know whether it due to over-eating or whether dropsy or some other fell disease struck him. I have not, however, narrated all. The smell was now almost insufferable for us and my mother fainted in the end of the house, her health having failed due to this new stench.

- If this pig is not put out of the house at once, said she feebly from the bed in the end of the house, I'll set these rushes on fire and then an end will be put to the hard life in this house of ours and even if we finish up later in hell, I've never heard there are pigs there anyway!

The Old-Fellow was puffing at the pipe strenuously in an attempt to fill the house with smoke as a defence against the stench. He replied to her:

- Woman! said he, the poor creature is sick and I'm slow to push him out and he without his health. 'Tis true that this stench is beyond all but don't you see that the pig himself is making no complaint, although he has a snout on him just like yourself there.

- He's dumb from the stench, said I.

- If that's the way it is, said my mother to the Old-Fellow, I'll put the rushes in flames!

The two of them continued nagging at one another for a long while but at last the Old-Fellow agreed to eject Ambrose. He went forward coaxing the pig to the door with whistling, nonsensical talk and pet-words but the beast stayed as he was, unmoved. It must have been that the pig's senses were deadened by the smell and that they failed to hear all the Old-Fellow had to say. At any rate, the Old-Fellow took a cudgel and drove the pig to the door—lifting him, beating him and pushing him with the weapon. When he reached the door it appeared to us that he was too fat to go out between the jambs. He was released and he returned to his fireside bed where he fell asleep.

- Upon me soul! said the Old-Grey-Fellow, but the creature is too well-fed and the doorway is too narrow although there is room in it for the horse himself.

- If that's the way it is, said my mother from the bed, then 'tis that way and it is hard to get away from what's in store for us.

Her voice was weak and low and I was certain that she was now willing to bow to fate, to the rottenness of the pig, and to face heaven. But suddenly a smothering fire arose in the end of the house—my mother burning the place. Back went the Old-Fellow in one leap, threw a couple of old sacks on the smoke and beat them with a big stick until the fire was quenched. He then beat my mother and gave her beneficial advice while doing so.

God bless us and save us! there was never as hard a life as that which Ambrose gave us for a fortnight after this. There is no describing the smell in our house. The pig was doubt-lessly ill and vapour arose from him reminiscent of a corpse unburied for a month. The house was rotten and putrid from top to bottom as a result of him. During that time my mother was in the end of the house unable to stand or speak. At the end of the fortnight, she bade us adieu and goodbye quietly and feebly and set her face towards eternity. The Old-Fellow was in the bed, smoking his pipe energetically during the night as a shield against the stench. He leapt up and dragged my mother out to the roadside, thus saving her from death that night although both of them were drenched to the skin. The following day the beds were put out by the road and the Old-Fellow said that there we would remain henceforth because, said he, it is better to be without house than life and even if we are drowned in the rain at night, that death itself is better than the other one within.

Martin O'Bannassa was going along the road that day and when he saw the unfragrant beds outside beneath the sky and our deserted house, he stopped and struck up a conversation with the Old-Fellow.

- 'Tis true that I don't understand life and the reason that the beds are outside, but look at the house on fire!

The Old-Fellow gazed at the house and shook his head.

- That's no fire, said he, but a rotten pig in our house. That's not smoke that's drifting from the house, as you think, Martin, but pig-steam.

- That steam is not pleasing to me, said Martin.

- There's no health in it! retorted the Old-Fellow.

Martin pondered the question for a while.

- It must be the way, said he, that this pig of yours is a pet and that you wouldn't want to cut his throat and bury him?

- 'Tis true indeed for you, Martin, said he.

- If that's the way, said Martin, I'll give ye help!

He went up on the roof of the house and put scraws of grass on the chimney-opening. He then closed the door and blocked the windows with mud and rags to keep air from going in or coming out.

- Now, said he, we must be quiet for an hour.

- Upon me soul, said the Old-Grey-Fellow, I don't understand this work but it's a wonderful world that's there today

♣ *When he reached the door it appeared to us that he was too fat to go out between the jambs. He was released and he returned to his fireside bed where he fell asleep.*

and if you're pleased with what you've done, I won't go against you.

At the end of that hour, Martin O'Bannassa opened the door and we all went in except my mother who was still weak and feeble on the damp rushes. Ambrose was stretched, cold and dead, on the hearth-stone. He had died of his own stench and a black cloud of smoke almost smothered us. The Old-Fellow was very sad but gave heartfelt thanks to Martin and ceased puffing his pipe for the first time in three months. Ambrose was buried in an honourable and becoming manner and we were all once more very well in that house. My mother recovered fast from her ill-health and was once more energetic, boiling large pots of potatoes for the other pigs.

Ambrose was an odd pig and I do not think that his like will be there again. Good luck to him if he be alive in another world today!

I WAS SEVEN years old when I was sent to school. I was tough, small and thin, wearing grey-wool breeches[1] but otherwise unclothed above and below. Many other children besides me were going to school that morning with the stain of the ashes still on the breeches of many of them. Some of them were crawling along the road, unable to walk. Many were from Dingle, some from Gweedore, another group floated in from Aran. All of us were strong and hearty on our first school day. A sod of turf was under the armpit of each one of us. Hearty and strong were we!

The master was named Osborne O'Loonassa. He was dark, spare and tall and unhealthy with a sharp, sour look on his face where the bones were protruding through the yellow skin. A ferocity of anger stood on his forehead as permanent as his hair and he cared not a whit for anyone.

We all gathered into the schoolhouse, a small unlovely hut where the rain ran down the walls and everything was soft and damp. We all sat on benches, without a word or a sound for fear of the master. He cast his venomous eyes over the room and they alighted on me where they stopped. By jove! I did not find his look pleasant while these two eyes were sifting me. After a while he directed a long yellow finger at me and said:

- Phwat is yer nam?

I did not understand what he said nor any other type of speech which is practised in foreign parts because I had only Gaelic as a mode of expression and as a protection against the difficulties of life. I could only stare at him, dumb with fear. I then saw a great fit of rage come over him and gradually increase exactly like a rain-cloud. I looked around timidly at the other boys. I heard a whisper at my back:

- Your name he wants!

My heart leaped with joy at this assistance and I was grateful to him who prompted me. I looked politely at the master and replied to him:

- Bonaparte, son of Michelangelo, son of Peter, son of Owen, son of Thomas's Sarah, grand-daughter of John's Mary, grand-daughter of James, son of Dermot . . .[2]

Before I had uttered or half-uttered my name, a rabid bark issued from the master and he beckoned to me with his finger. By the time I had reached him, he had an oar in his grasp. Anger had come over him in a flood-tide at this stage and he had a businesslike grip of the oar in his two hands. He drew it over his shoulder and brought it down hard upon me with a swish of air, dealing me a destructive blow on the skull. I fainted from that blow but before I became totally unconscious I heard him scream:

- Yer nam, said he, is Jams O'Donnell![3]

Jams O'Donnell? These two words were singing in my ears when feeling returned to me. I found that I was lying on my side on the floor, my breeches, hair and all my person saturated with the streams of blood which flowed from the split caused by the oar in my skull. When my eyes were in operation again, there was another youngster on his feet being asked his name. It was apparent that this child lacked shrewdness completely and had not drawn good beneficial lessons for himself from the beating which I had received because he replied to the master, giving his common name as I had. The master again brandished the oar which was in his grasp and did not cease until he was shedding blood plentifully, the youngster being left unconscious and stretched out on the floor, a bloodied bundle. And during the beating the master screamed once more:

‐ Yer nam is Jams O'Donnell!

He continued in this manner until every creature in the school had been struck down by him and all had been named *Jams O'Donnell*. No young skull in the countryside that day remained unsplit. Of course, there were many unable to walk by the afternoon and were transported home by relatives. It was a pitiable thing for those who had to swim back to Aran that evening and were without a bite of food or a sup of milk since morning.

When I myself reached home, my mother was there boiling potatoes for the pigs and I asked her for a couple for lunch. I received them and ate them with only a little pinch of salt. The bad situation in the school was bothering me all this time and I decided to question my mother.

‐ Woman, said I, I've heard that every fellow in this place is called *Jams O'Donnell*. If that's the way it is, it's a wonderful world we have and isn't O'Donnell the wonderful man and the number of children he has?

‐ 'Tis true for you, said she.

‐ If 'tis true itself, said I, I've no understanding of that same truth.

‐ If that's the way, said she, don't you understand that it's

He drew it over his shoulder and brought it down hard upon me with a h *of air, dealing me a destructive blow on the skull.*

Gaels that live in this side of the country and that they can't escape from fate? It was always said and written that every Gaelic youngster is hit on his first school day because he doesn't understand English and the foreign form of his name and that no one has any respect for him because he's Gaelic to the marrow. There's no other business going on in school that day but punishment and revenge and the same fooling about *Jams O'Donnell*. Alas! I don't think that there'll ever be any good settlement for the Gaels but only hardship for them always. The Old-Grey-Fellow was also hit one day of his life and called *Jams O'Donnell* as well.

- Woman, said I, what you say is amazing and I don't think I'll ever go back to that school but it's now the end of my learning!

- You're shrewd, said she, in your early youth.

I had no other connection with education from that day onwards and therefore my Gaelic skull has not been split since. But seven years afterwards (when I was seven years older), it came to pass that wonderful things happened in our neighbourhood, things connected with the question of learning and, for this reason, I must present some little account of them here.

The Old-Fellow was one day in Dingle buying tobacco and tasting spirits, when he heard news which amazed him. He did not believe it because he never trusted the people of that town. The next day he was selling herrings in the Rosses and had the same news from them there; he then half-accepted the story but did not altogether swallow it. The third day he was in Galway city and the story was there likewise. At last he believed it believingly and when he returned, drenched and wet (the downpour comes heavily on us unfailingly each night), he informed my mother of the matter (and me also who was eavesdropping in the end of the house!).

- Upon me soul, said he, I hear that the English Government is going to do great work for the good of the paupers here in this place, safe and saved may everyone be in this house! It is fixed to pay the likes of us two pounds a skull for every child of ours that speaks English instead of this thieving Gaelic. Trying to separate us from the Gaelic they are, praise be to them sempiternally! I don't think there'll ever be good conditions for the Gaels while having small houses in the corner of the glen, going about in the dirty ashes, constantly fishing in the constant storm, telling stories at night about the hardships and hard times of the Gaels in sweet words of Gaelic is natural to them.

- Woe is me! exclaimed my mother, and I with only the one son; this dying example here that's on his backside over on the floor there.

- If that's the way, said the Old-Fellow, you'll have more children or else you're without resource!

During the following week, a staunch black gloom came over the Old-Grey-Fellow, a portent that his mind was filled with difficult complicated thoughts while he endeavoured to solve the question of the want of children. One day, while in Cahirciveen, he heard that the new scheme was under way; that the good foreign money had been received already in many houses in that district and that an inspector was going about through the countryside counting the children and testing the quality of English they had. He also heard that this inspector was an aged crippled man without good sight and that he lacked enthusiasm for his work as well. The Old-Fellow pondered all that he heard and when he returned at night (drenched and wet), he informed us that there is no cow unmilkable, no hound unraceable and, also, no money which cannot be stolen.

- Upon me soul, said he, we'll have the full of the house

before morning and everyone of them earning two pounds for us.

 - It's a wonderful world, said my mother, but I'm not expecting anything of that kind and neither did I hear that a house could be filled in one night.

 - Don't forget, said he, that Sarah is here.

 - Sarah, indeed! said my startled mother.

Amazement leaped up and down through me when I heard the mention of the sow's name.

 - The same lady exactly, said he. She has a great crowd of a family at present and they have vigorous voices, even though their dialect is unintelligible to us. How do we know but that their conversation isn't in English. Of course, youngsters and piglets have the same habits and take notice that there's a close likeness between their skins.

 - You're reflective, replied my mother, but they must have suits of clothes made for them before the inspector comes to look at them.

 - They must indeed, said the Old-Grey-Fellow.

 - It's a wonderful world these days, said I from the back-bed at the end of the house.

 - Upon me soul, but 'tis wonderful, said the Old-Fellow, but in spite of the payment of this English money for the good of our likes, I don't think there'll ever be good conditions for the Gaels.

The following day we had these particular residents within, each one wearing a grey-wool clothing while squealing, rooting, grunting and snoring in the rushes in the back of the house. A blind man would know of their presence from the stench there. Whatever the condition of the Gaels was at that time, our own condition was not at all good while these fellows were our constant company.

We kept a good vigil for the inspector's arrival. We were obliged to wait quite a while for him but, as the Old-Fellow said, whatever is coming will come. The inspector approached us on a rainy day when there was bad light everywhere and a heavy twilight in the end of our house where the pigs were. Whoever said that the inspector was old and feeble, told the truth. He was English and had little health, the poor fellow! He was thin, stooped and sour-faced. He cared not a whit for the Gaels—no wonder!—and never had any desire to go into the cabins where they lived. When he came to us, he stopped at the threshold and peered short-sightedly into the house. He was startled when he noticed the smell we had but did not depart because he had much experience of the habitations of the true Gaels. The Old-Grey-Fellow stood respectfully and politely near the door in front of the gentleman, I beside him and my mother was in the back of the house caring and petting the piglets. Occasionally, a piglet jumped into the centre of the floor and without delay returned to the twilight. One might have thought that he was a strong male youngster, crawling through the house because of the breeches which he wore. A murmur of talk arose all this time from my mother and the piglets; it was difficult to understand because of the noise of wind and rain outside. The gentleman looked sharply about him, deriving but little pleasure from the stench. At last he spoke:

- How many?
- Twalf, sor!⁴ said the Old-Grey-Fellow courteously.
- Twalf?

The other man threw another quick glance at the back of the house while he considered and attempted to find some explanation for the speech he heard.

- All spik Inglish?
- All spik, sor, said the Old-Fellow.

Then the gentleman noticed me standing behind the Old-Grey-Fellow and he spoke gruffly to me:

- Phwat is yer nam? said he.

- Jams O'Donnell, sor!

It was apparent that neither I nor my like appealed to this elegant stranger but this answer delighted him because he could now declare that he questioned the young folk and was answered in sweet English; the last of his labours was completed and he might now escape freely from the stench. He departed amid the rain-showers without word or blessing for us. The Old-Grey-Fellow was well satisfied with what we had accomplished and I had a fine meal of potatoes as a reward from him. The pigs were driven out and we were all quiet and happy for the day. Some days afterwards the Old-Grey-Fellow received a yellow letter and there was a big currency note within it. That is another story and I shall narrate it at another time in this volume.

When the inspector had gone and the pigs' odour cleared from the house, it appeared to us that the end of that work was done and the termination of that course reached by us. But, alas! things are not what they seem and if a stone be cast, there is no foreknowledge of where it may land. On the following day, when we counted the pigs while divesting them of their breeches, it appeared that we were missing one. Great was the lamentation of the Old-Grey-Fellow when he noticed that both pig and suit of clothes had been snatched privily from him in the quiet of the night. It is true that he often stole a neighbour's pig and he often stated that he never slaughtered one of his own but sold them all, although we always had half-sides of bacon in our house. Night and day there was constant thieving in progress in the parish—paupers impoverishing each other—but no one stole a pig except the Old-Fellow. Of course, it was not joy which flooded his heart when he found another person playing his own tune.

- Upon me soul, said he to me, I'm afraid they're not all just and honest around here. I wouldn't mind about the young little pig but there was a fine bit of stuff in that breeches.

- Everyone to his own opinion, my good man, said I, but I don't think that anyone took that pig or the breeches either.

- Do you think, said he, that fear would keep them from doing the stealing?

- No, I replied, but the stench would.

- I don't know, son, said he, but that you're truly in the right. I don't know but that the pig is off rambling?

- It's an unfragrant rambling if 'tis true for you, my good man, said I.

That night the Old-Fellow stole a pig from Martin O'Bannassa and killed it quietly in the end of the house. It happened that the conversation had reminded him that our bacon was in short supply. No further discussion concerning the lost pig took place then.

A new month called March was born; remained with us for a month and then departed. At the end of that time we heard a loud snorting one night in the height of the rain. The Old-Fellow thought that yet another pig was being snatched from him by force and went out. When he returned, his companion consisted of none other than our missing pig, drenched and wet, the fine breeches about him in saturated rags. The creature seemed by his appearance to have trudged quite an area of the earth that night. My mother arose willingly when the Old-Fellow stated that it was necessary to prepare a large pot of potatoes for the one who had after all returned. The awakening of the household did not agree too well with Charlie and, having lain awake, looking furious during the talking and confusion, he suddenly arose and charged out into the rain. The poor creature never favoured socialising much. God bless him!

The return in darkness of the pig was amazing but still more amazing was the news which he imparted to us when

♣ *Suddenly he noticed a commotion at the doorway. Then, by the weak light of the fire, he saw the door being pushed in (it was never equipped with a bolt) and in came a poor old man, drenched and wet, drunk to the full of his skin and creeping instead of walking upright because of the drunkenness. The creature was lost without delay in the darkness of the house but wherever he lay on the floor, the gentleman's heart leaped when he heard a great flow of talk issuing from that place. It really was rapid, complicated, stern speech—one might have thought the old fellow was swearing drunkenly—but the gentleman did not tarry to understand it. He leaped up and set the machine near the one who was spewing out Gaelic.*

he had partaken of the potatoes, having been stripped of the breeches by the Old-Grey-Fellow. The Old-Fellow found a pipe with a good jot of tobacco in one pocket. In another he found a shilling and a small bottle of spirits.

- Upon me soul, said he, if 'tis hardship that's always in store for the Gaels, it's not that way with this creature. Look, said he, directing his attention to the pig, where did you get these articles, sir?

The pig threw a sharp glance out of his two little eyes at the Old-Fellow but did not reply.

- Leave the breeches on him, said my mother. How do we know but that he'll be coming to us every week and wonderful precious things in his pockets—pearls, necklaces, snuff and maybe a money-note—wherever in Ireland he can get them. Isn't it a marvellous world today altogether?

- How do we know, said the Old-Grey-Fellow in reply to her, that he will ever again return but live where he can get these good things and we'd be for ever without the fine suit of clothes that he has?

- True for you, indeed, alas! said my mother.

The pig was now stark naked and was put with the others.

A full month went by before we received an explanation of the complicated matter of that night. The Old-Fellow heard a whisper in Galway, half a word in Gweedore and a phrase in Dunquin. He synthesised them all and one afternoon, when the day was done and the nocturnal downpour was mightily upon us, he told the following interesting story.

There was a gentleman from Dublin travelling through the country who was extremely interested in Gaelic. The gentleman understood that in Corkadoragha there were people alive who were unrivalled in any other region and also that their likes would never be there again. He had an instrument called a gramophone[5] and this instrument was capable of memorising all it heard if anyone narrated stories

or old lore to it; it could also spew out all it had heard whenever one desired it. It was a wonderful instrument and
frightened many people in the area and struck others dumb;
it is doubtful whether its like will ever be there again. Since
folks thought that it was unlucky; the gentleman had a
difficult task collecting the folklore tales from them.

For that reason, he did not attempt to collect the folklore
of our ancients and our ancestors except under cover of
darkness when both he and the instrument were hidden in
the end of a cabin and both of them listening intently. It was
evident that he was a wealthy person because he spent much
money on spirits every night to remove the shyness and
disablement from the old people's tongues. He had that
reputation throughout the countryside and whenever it
became known that he was visiting in Jimmy's or Jimmy
Tim Pat's[6] house, every old fellow who lived within a
radius of five miles hastened there to seek tongue-loosening
from this fiery liquid medicine; it must be mentioned that
many of the youths accompanied them.

On the night of which we speak, the gentleman was in the
house of Maximilian O'Penisa quietly resting in the darkness
and with the hearing-machine by him. There were at least
a hundred old fellows gathered in around him, sitting,
dumb and invisible, in the shadow of the walls and passing
around the gentleman's bottles of spirits from one to the
other. Sometimes a little spell of weak whispering was
audible but generally no sound except the roar of the water
falling outside from the gloomy skies, just as if those on high
were emptying buckets of that vile wetness on the world. If
the spirits loosened the men's tongues, it did not result in
talk but rather in rolling and tasting on their lips the bright
drops of spirits. Time went by in that manner and it was
rather late in the night. As a result of both the heavy silence
inside and the hum of the rain outside, the gentleman was

becoming a little disheartened. He had not collected one of the gems of our ancients that night and had lost spirits to the value of five pounds without result.

Suddenly he noticed a commotion at the doorway. Then, by the weak light of the fire, he saw the door being pushed in (it was never equipped with a bolt) and in came a poor old man, drenched and wet, drunk to the full of his skin and creeping instead of walking upright because of the drunkenness. The creature was lost without delay in the darkness of the house but wherever he lay on the floor, the gentleman's heart leaped when he heard a great flow of talk issuing from that place. It really was rapid, complicated, stern speech— one might have thought that the old fellow was swearing drunkenly—but the gentleman did not tarry to understand it. He leaped up and set the machine near the one who was spewing out Gaelic. It appeared that the gentleman thought the Gaelic extremely difficult and he was overjoyed that the machine was absorbing it; he understood that good Gaelic is difficult but that the best Gaelic of all is well-nigh unintelligible. After about an hour the stream of talk ceased. The gentleman was pleased with the night's business. As a token of his gratitude he put a white pipe, a jot of tobacco and a little bottle of spirits in the old fellow's pocket who was now in an inebriated slumber where he had fallen. Then the gentleman departed homewards in the rain with the machine, leaving them his blessing quietly but no one responded to it because drunkenness had come in a flood-tide now through the skull of everyone of them who was present.

It was said later in the area that the gentleman was highly praised for the lore which he had stored away in the hearing-machine that night. He journeyed to Berlin, a city of Germany in Europe, and narrated all that the machine had heard in the presence of the most learned ones of the Continent. These learned ones said that they never heard any fragment of Gaelic which was so good, so poetic and so obscure as it and that were sure there was no fear for Gaelic while the like was audible in Ireland. They bestowed fondly a fine academic degree on the gentleman and, something more interesting still, they appointed a small committee of their own members to make a detailed study of the language of the machine to determine whether any sense might be made of it.

I do not know whether it was Gaelic or English or a strange irregular dialect which was in the old speech which the gentleman collected from among us here in Corkadoragha but it is certain that whatever word was uttered that night, came from our rambling pig.

Chapter 4

The comings and goings of the Gaeligores ♣ **the Gaelic college** ♣
a Gaelic feis in our countryside ♣ **the gentlemen from Dublin** ♣
sorrow follows the jollity

O NE AFTERNOON I was reclining on the rushes in the end of the house considering the ill-luck and evil that had befallen the Gaels (and would always abide with them) when the Old-Grey-Fellow came in the door. He appeared terrified, a severe fit of trembling throughout his body and limbs, his tongue between his teeth dry and languid and bereft of vigour. I forget whether he sat or fell but he alighted on the floor near me with a terrible thump which set the house dancing. Then he began to wipe away the large beads of sweat which were on his face.

- Welcome, my good man! said I gently, and also may health and longevity be yours! I've just been thinking of the pitiable situation of the Gaels at present and also that they're not all in the same state; I perceive that yourself are in a worse situation than any Gael since the commencement of the reign of Gaelicism. It appears that you're bereft of vigour?

- I am, said he.

- You're worried?

- I am.

- And is it the way, said I, that new hardships and new calamities are in store for the Gaels and a new overthrow is destined for the little green country which is the native land of both of us?

The Old-Grey-Fellow heaved a sigh and a sad withdrawn appearance spread over his face, leading me to understand that he was meditating on eternity itself. He did not reply to me but his lips were dry and his voice weak and feeble.

- Little son, said he, I don't think that the coming night's rain will drench anyone because the end of the world will arrive before that very night. The signs are there in plenty through the firmament. Today I saw the first ray of sunshine ever to come to Corkadoragha, an unworldly shining a hundred times more venomous than the fire and it glaring down from the skies upon me and coming with a needle's sharpness at my eyes. I also saw a breeze going across the grass of a field and returning when it reached the other side. I heard a crow screeching in the field with a pig's voice, a blackbird bellowing and a bull whistling. I must say that these frightening things don't predict good news. Bad and all as they were, I heard another thing that put a hell of fright in my heart . . .

- All that you say is wonderful, loving fellow, said I honestly, and a little account of that other sign would be nice.

The Old-Fellow was silent for a while and when he withdrew from that taciturnity, he did not produce speech but a hoarse whispering into my ear.

- I was coming home today from Ventry, said he, and I noticed a strange, elegant, well-dressed gentleman coming towards me along the road. Since I'm a well-mannered Gael, into the ditch with me so as to leave all the road to the gentleman and not have me there before him, putrifying the public road. But alas! there's no explaining the world's wonders! When he came as far as me and I standing there humbly in the dung and filth of the bottom of the ditch, what would you say but didn't he stop and, looking fondly at me, *didn't he speak to me!*

Amazed and terrified, I exhaled all the air in my lungs. I was then dumb with terror for a little while.

- But . . . said the Old-Fellow, laying a trembling hand upon my person, dumb also but making the utmost endeavour to regain his power of speech, but . . . wait! *He spoke to me in Gaelic!*

When I had heard all this, I became suspicious. I thought that the Old-Fellow was romancing or raving in a drunken delirium . . . There are things beyond the bounds of credibility.

- If 'tis true for you, said I, we'll never live another night and without a doubt, the end of the world is here today.

It is, however, mysterious and bewildering how the human being comes free from every peril. That night arrived both safely and punctually and in spite of all, we were safe. Another thing: as the days went by, it was evident that the Old-Fellow spoke the truth about the gentleman who addressed him in Gaelic. Oftentimes now there were gentlemen to be seen about the roads, some young and others aged, addressing the poor Gaels in awkward unintelligible Gaelic and delaying them on their way to the field. The gentlemen had fluent English from birth but they never practised this noble tongue in the presence of the Gaels lest, it seemed, the Gaels might pick up an odd word of it as a protection against the difficulties of life. That is how the group, called the Gaeligores nowadays, came to Corkadoragha for the first time. They rambled about the countryside with little black notebooks for a long time before the people noticed that they were not *peelers* but gentle-folk endeavouring to learn the Gaelic of our ancestors and ancients. As each year went by, these folk became more numerous. Before long the place was dotted with them. With the passage of time, the advent of spring was no longer judged by the flight of the first swallow but by the first Gaeligore seen on the roads. They brought happiness and money and high revelry with them when they came; pleasant and funny were these creatures, God bless them! and I think that their likes will not be there again!

When they had been coming to us for about ten years or thereabouts, we noticed that their number among us was diminishing and that those who remained faithful to us were lodging in Galway and in Rannafast while making day-trips to Corkadoragha. Of course, they carried away much of our good Gaelic when they departed from us each night but they left few pennies as recompense to the paupers who waited for them and had kept the Gaelic tongue alive for such as them a thousand years. People found this difficult to understand; it had always been said that accuracy of Gaelic (as well as holiness of spirit) grew in proportion to one's lack of worldly goods and since we had the choicest poverty and calamity, we did not understand why the scholars were interested in any half-awkward, perverse Gaelic which was audible in other parts. The Old-Grey-Fellow discussed this matter with a noble Gaeligore whom he met.

- Why and wherefore, said he, are the learners leaving us? Is it the way that they've left so much money with us in the last ten years that they have relieved the hunger of the countryside and that for this reason, our Gaelic has declined?

- I don't think that Father Peter[1] has the word *decline* in any of his works, said the Gaeligore courteously.

The Old-Grey-Fellow did not reply to this sentence but he probably made a little speech quietly for his own ear.

- 'He struck out by the doorway' - do you use that sentence? said the Gaeligore.

- Forget it, boy! said the Old-Fellow and left him with the question still unsolved in his skull.

In spite of it all, he succeeded in solving that difficulty. It was explained to him—no one knows by whom, but it was someone with little Gaelic who was there—it was explained what was upside-down and amiss and back-to-front with Corkadoragha as a centre of learning. It appeared that:

1. The tempest of the countryside was too tempestuous.
2. The putridity of the countryside was too putrid.
3. The poverty of the countryside was too poor.
4. The Gaelicism of the countryside was too Gaelic.
5. The tradition of the countryside was too traditional.

When the Old-Fellow realised that matters were thus, he pondered the matter in his mind for a week. He saw that the learners were in danger of death from the constant vomiting and spite of the sky; that they could not take shelter in the people's dwellings because of the stench and smell of the pigs. By the end of the week, it seemed to him that everything would be satisfactory if we had a college as there was in the Rosses and Connemara. He pondered this intensely for another week and at the end of that time all was clear and definite in his own mind; we should have a big Gaelic feis in Corkadoragha to collect the money for the college. That very night he visited some respectable people in Letter-kenny to arrange the managements and details of the feis; before morning he was about the same business in the Great Blasket and, meanwhile, he had sent important letters to Dublin, using the post-mistress as an amanuensis. Of course, there was no one in Ireland as eager in the Gaelic cause as the Old-Grey-Fellow was that night; that the college was built finally on the Old-Fellow's land was no wonder; land which was extremely high-priced when it was bought from him! The feis itself was held in his own field and he received two days' rent for the little plot where the platform stood. If pennies are falling, he often said, see to it that they fall into your own pocket; you won't sin by covetousness if you have all the money in your own possession.

Yes! we shall never forget the feis of Corkadoragha and the revelry that was ours during it. The night beforehand a large gang of men worked diligently in the midst of the rain erecting a platform at the gable-end of our house while the Old-Fellow stood on the door-step, dry from the rain, directing the work by instruction and good counsel. None of these fellows ever had good health again after the downpour and storm of that night, while one of those who did not survive was buried before that platform was dismantled on which he had laid down his life for the cause of the Gaelic language. May he be safe today on the platform of heaven for ever. Amen.

At this time, I was about fifteen years of age, an unhealthy, dejected, broken-toothed youth, growing with a rapidity which left me weak and without good health. I think I never remember before or since so many strangers and gentlemen coming together in one place in Ireland. Crowds came from Dublin and Galway city, all with respectable, well-made clothes on them; an occasional fellow without any breeches on him but wearing a lady's underskirt instead. It was stated that such as he wore Gaelic costume and, if this was correct, what a peculiar change came in your appearance as a result of a few Gaelic words in your head! There were men present wearing a simple unornamented dress—these, I thought, had little Gaelic; others had such nobility, style and elegance in their feminine attire that it was evident that their Gaelic was fluent. I felt quite ashamed that there was not even one true

Gael among us in Corkadoragha. They had yet another distinction which we did not have since we lost true Gaelicism —they all lacked names and surnames but received honorary titles, self-granted, which took their style from the sky and the air, the farm and the storm, field and fowl. There was a bulky, fat, slow-moving man whose face was grey and flabby and appeared suspended between deaths from two mortal diseases; he took unto himself the title of *The Gaelic Daisy*. Another poor fellow whose size and energy were that of the mouse, called himself *The Sturdy Bull*. As well as these, the following gentlemen were also present as I remember:

> Connacht Cat
> The Little Brown Hen
> The Bold Horse
> The Gaudy Crow
> The Running Knight
> Roseen of the Hill
> Goll Mac Morna
> Popeye the Sailor
> The Humble Bishop
> The Sweet Blackbird
> Mary's Spinning-wheel
> The Sod of Turf
> Baboro
> My Friend Drumroosk[2]
> The Oar
> The Other Beetle
> The Skylark
> The Robin Redbreast
> The Bout of Dancing
> The Bandy Ulsterman
> The Slim Fox
> The Sea-cat

The Branchy Tree
The West Wind
The Temperate Munsterman
William the Sailor
The White Egg
Eight Men
Tim the Blacksmith
The Purple Cock
The Little Stack of Barley
The Dative Case
Silver
The Speckled Fellow
The Headache
The Lively Boy
The Gluttonous Rabbit
The High Hat
John of the Glen
Yours respectfully
The Little Sweet Kiss

The morning of the feis was cold and stormy without halt
or respite from the nocturnal downpour. We had all arisen
at cockcrow and had partaken of potatoes before daybreak.
During the night the Gaelic paupers had been assembling
in Corkadoragha from every quarter of the Gaeltacht and,
upon my soul, ragged and hungry was the group we saw
before us when we arose. They had potatoes and turnips in
their pockets and consumed them greedily in the feis-field;
as beverage afterwards they had the rainwater. It was high
morning before the gentle-folk arrived because the bad
roads had delayed their motor-cars. When the first motor
came in view, many paupers were terrified by it; they ran
from it with sharp screams and hid among the rocks but
issued forth again boldly when they saw there was no harm

whatever in those new-fangled machines. The Old-Grey-Fellow welcomed the noble Gaels from Dublin and offered them a drink of buttermilk as a mark of respect and as a nourishing potion after their journey. They withdrew then to arrange the details of the function and to elect feis-officers. When they had done, the assembly was informed that the Gaelic Daisy had been elected President of the Feis, the Eager Cat as Vice-President, the Dative Case as Auditor, the West Wind as Secretary and the Old-Grey-Fellow as Treasurer. After another bout of discussion and conversation, the President and the other great bucks climbed up on the platform in the presence of the populace and then the Grand Feis of Corkadoragha commenced. The President placed a yellow watch on the table before him, stuck his thumbs into the armpits of his waistcoat and delivered this truly Gaelic oration:

- Gaels! he said, it delights my Gaelic heart to be here today speaking Gaelic with you at this Gaelic feis in the centre of the Gaeltacht. May I state that I am a Gael. I'm Gaelic from the crown of my head to the soles of my feet—Gaelic front and back, above and below. Likewise, you are all truly Gaelic. We are all Gaelic Gaels of Gaelic lineage. He who is Gaelic, will be Gaelic evermore. I myself have spoken not a word except Gaelic since the day I was born—just like you— and every sentence I've ever uttered has been on the subject of Gaelic. If we're truly Gaelic, we must constantly discuss the question of the Gaelic revival and the question of Gaelicism. There is no use in having Gaelic, if we converse in it on non-Gaelic topics. He who speaks Gaelic but fails to discuss the language question is not truly Gaelic in his heart; such conduct is of no benefit to Gaelicism because he only jeers at Gaelic and reviles the Gaels. There is nothing in this life so nice and so Gaelic as truly true Gaelic Gaels who speak in true Gaelic Gaelic about the truly Gaelic language. I hereby declare this feis to be Gaelically open! Up the Gaels! Long live the Gaelic tongue!

When this noble Gael sat down on his Gaelic backside, a great tumult and hand-clapping arose throughout the assembly. Many of the native Gaels were becoming feeble from standing because their legs were debilitated from lack of nourishment, but they made no complaint. Then the Eager Cat stepped forward, a tall, broad, self-confident man whose face was dark blue from the frequent shaving of his abundant facial hair. He delivered himself of another finer oration:

– Gaels! said he, I bid you heartily welcome here to this feis today and I wish good health, long life, success and prosperity to each and every one of you until the crack of doom and while Gaels are alive in Ireland. Gaelic is our native language and we must, therefore, be in earnest about Gaelic. I don't think the Government is in earnest about Gaelic. I don't think they're Gaelic at heart. They jeer at Gaelic and revile the Gaels. We must all be strongly in favour of Gaelic. Likewise, I don't think the university is in earnest about Gaelic. The commercial and industrial classes are not in favour of Gaelic. I often wonder whether *anyone* is in earnest about Gaelic. No liberty without unity! Long live our Gaelic tongue!

– No liberty without royalty![3] said the Old-Grey-Fellow in my ear. He always had great respect for the King of England.

– It appears, said I, that this Gaelic gentleman is fully in earnest about Gaelic?

– Apparently he's too well nourished in the upper part of his head, said the Old-Grey-Fellow.

Not only one fine oration followed this one but eight. Many Gaels collapsed from hunger and from the strain of listening while one fellow died most Gaelically in the midst of the assembly. Yes! we had a great day of oratory in Corkadoragha that day!

♣ *Not only one fine oration followed this one but eight. Many Gaels collapsed from hunger and from the strain of listening while one fellow died most Gaelically in the midst of the assembly. Yes! we had a great day of oratory in Corkadoragha that day!*

When the last word had been said from the platform about Gaelic, the revelry and tumult of the feis began. The President presented a silver medal as prize for him who was most in earnest about Gaelic. Five competitors, who sat together on a wall, were entered for that competition. Early in the day they commenced speaking Gaelic with all their might and without interruption in the stream of talking, while they discoursed only about Gaelic. I never heard such rapid, sturdy, strong Gaelic as this flood-tide which poured down upon us from the wall. For three hours or thereabouts, the speech was sweet and the words recognisable, one from the other. By afternoon the sweetness and the sense had almost completely departed from it and all that was audible were nonsensical chatterings and rough inarticulate grunts. At fall of darkness one man collapsed on the ground, another fell asleep (but not silent!) and a third fellow was borne home, stricken by brain-fever which carried him off to the other life before morning. That left two of them bleating feebly by the wall with the nocturnal rains pouring down on them destructively. Midnight had come before the competition really ended. One of the men halted suddenly the sound that was ramblingly issuing from him and the other one was presented with the silver medal by the President and also with a fine oration. As to the other one who lost in the contest, he has never spoken since that night and he will never certainly speak again. All the Gaelic which he had in his head, said the Old-Grey-Fellow, he has spoken it to-night! As to the rogue who won the medal, he set his house on fire while he himself was within exactly one year after the feis-day and neither he nor his house have been seen after that conflagration. Wherever their habitation be today, in Ireland or on high, safe may be the five men who competed for the medal that day!

Eight more died on that same day from excess of dancing

and scarcity of food. The Dublin gentlemen said that no Gaelic dance was as Gaelic as the Long Dance, that it was Gaelic according to its length and truly Gaelic whenever it was truly long. Whatever the length of time needed for the longest Long Dance, it is certain that it was trivial in comparison with the task we had in Corkadoragha on that day. The dance continued until the dancers drove their lives out through the soles of their feet and eight died during the course of the feis. Due to both the fatigue caused by the revels and the truly Gaelic famine that was ours always, they could not be succoured when they fell on the rocky dancing floor and, upon my soul, short was their tarrying on this particular area because they wended their way to eternity without more ado.

Even though death snatched many fine people from us, the events of the feis went on sturdily and steadily, we were ashamed to be considered not strongly in favour of Gaelic while the President's eye was upon us. As far east and west as the eye might rove, there were men and women, young and old, dancing, hopping and twisting distressingly in a manner which recalled to one a windy afternoon at sea.

A peculiar little incident took place at the coming of twilight when the people had spent the whole day dancing and no one had a scrap of skin under his feet. The President graciously permitted a five-minute break and all dropped down gratefully on the damp ground. After the break, the Eight-Hand Reel was announced and I noticed the gentleman entitled Eight Men swallowing fiercely from a bottle which he had in his pocket. When the Eight-Hand Reel was announced, he threw away the bottle and went on alone to the dancing place. Others followed him to step it out in his company but he threatened them angrily, shouted that the house was full and made a violent foray with his boot on anyone who came near him. Before long, he was really frenzied and was not quietened until a terrible blow was struck on the back of his head by a large stone. I never yet saw anyone so bold, uppish and unmanageable as he was before he was struck or so peaceable and quiet after the casting of the stone by the Old-Grey-Fellow. Doubtless, a few words often lead a man astray.

As to myself, I never ceased until I reached the magic bottle, thrown aside by Eight Men. There was a fine nip still in it and by the time I had this in my stomach, a remarkable change had come over the world. The air was sweet, the appearance of the countryside had improved and there was pleasure of heart in the very rain. I sat down on the fence and sang a Gaelic song at the top of my voice, accompanying the tune with the jingle of the empty bottle on the stones. When I had finished the song and looked over my shoulder, I saw none other than Eight Men stretched out in the muck with blood dripping profusely from the hole made by the stone. If he was really alive, then it was evident that life was not very vigorous within him and I was of the opinion that he was in danger of imminent dissolution. 'If he is departing from us,' said I to myself, 'he won't be able to take to the place beyond any other bottle he has to drink.' I leaped over the fence, bent down and ran my fingers inquisitively over the gentleman. Before long I discovered another little bottle of the ardent water and may I say that I neither made stay or delay until I was in a secluded place while my throat was being scorched by that oil of the sun. Of course, I did not have any training in toping at that time, not even knowledge of what I was about. If the bare truth be told, I did not prosper very well. My senses went astray, evidently. Misadventure fell on my misfortune, a further misadventure fell on that misadventure and before long the misadventures were falling thickly on the first misfortune and on myself. Then a shower of misfortunes fell on the misadventures, heavy misadventures fell on the misfortunes after that and finally one great brown misadventure came upon everything, quenching the light and stopping the course of life.[4] I did not feel anything for a long while; I did not see anything, neither did I hear a sound. Unknown to me, the earth was revolving on its course through the firmament. It was a week before I felt that a stir of life was still within me and a fortnight before I was completely certain that I was alive. A half-year went by before I had recovered fully from the ill-health which that night's business had bestowed on me, God give us all grace! I did not notice the second day of the feis.

Yes! I think that I shall never forget the Gaelic feis which we had in Corkadoragha. During the course of the feis many died whose likes will not be there again and, had the feis continued a week longer, no one would be alive now in Corkadoragha in all truth. Apart from the malady which I contracted from the bottle and the amazing weird things which I saw, there is one other matter that fixes the day of the feis firmly in my memory: from that day forward the Old-Grey-Fellow was in possession of a yellow watch!

ONCE UPON a time when the potatoes were becoming scarce in our house and we were worried by the shadow of famine, the Old-Grey-Fellow announced that it was timely for us to go hunting if we desired to keep our souls within our bodies instead of permitting them to fly out into the firmament like the little melodious birds.

– 'Tis no good for the people to be living in the shadow of one another if all that's left of them is shadows.[1] I never did hear that anyone's shadow was effective as a shelter against the hunger.

I certainly derived but little pleasure of heart from this conversation. At this time I was almost twenty years old and one of the laziest and most indolent persons living in Ireland. I had no experience of work and neither had I found any desire for it ever since the day I was born. I had never been out in the field. I was of the opinion that hunting entailed particular hardship: perpetual moving in the heart of the hills, perpetual watchfulness while stretched out in the damp grass, perpetual hiding, perpetual fatigue; I would have been satisfied without any hunting while I lived.

- Where in Ireland, do you think, sir, said I, is the best hunting to be found?

- Oh little teeny weeny son, said he, it's in the Rosses in Donegal that the best hunting is to be found and every other thing in that place is excellent also.

The melancholy almost lifted from me when I heard that we were going towards the Rosses. I never was in that part of the country but I had heard so much from the Old-Fellow concerning it that I had desired for a long time to go there; if I had had the choice, I am not certain whether I should have preferred to journey to heaven or to the Rosses. You might have thought from the Old-Fellow's conversation that your bargain would be better if you went to the Rosses. It is hardly necessary to state that the same gentleman had been reared in the Rosses.

According to what I had heard, he was the best man in the Rosses during his youth. There was no one in the country-side comparable to him where jumping, ransacking, fishing, love-making, drinking, thieving, fighting, ham-stringing, cattle-running, swearing, gambling, night-walking, hunting, dancing, boasting and stick-fighting were concerned.

He alone killed Martyn in Gweedore in 1889 when the aforesaid person attempted to take Father MacFadden a prisoner to Derry; he alone assassinated Lord Leitrim near Cratlough in 1875; he alone first inscribed his name in Gaelic on any cart and was prosecuted on that historic occasion; he alone founded the Land League, the Fenians and the Gaelic League. Yes! he had had a busy broad life and it had been of great benefit to Ireland. Were it not that he was born when he was and led the life he had, conversational subjects would be scarce among us today in this country.

- Will we be looking for rabbits? said I most politely.
- We won't! said he, or if you wish: We wull na!
- Crabs or lobsters?
- Naw!
- Wild pigs?
- They're not pigs and they're not wild! said he.
- If that's the way, sir, said I, come along and I won't put any more questions on you for the present because you're not too talkative.

We left my mother snoozing in the rushes behind us and we moved off in the direction of the Rosses.

On the road we met a man from the Rosses named Jams O'Donnell and we saluted him kindly. He stopped in front of us, recited the Lay of Victories, walked three steps of mercy with us, took a tongs from his pocket and threw it after us. In addition to that, he had the appearance of one who had a five-noggin bottle in his pocket as well and had a pledge of hand and word with a maiden in Glendown. He lived in a corner of the glen on your right-hand side as you go eastward along the road. It was evident that he was Ultonian according to the formula in the good books. He was an old-timer and rebellious.

- Are you very well? said the Old-Fellow.
- I'm only middling, said Jams, and I've no Gaelic, only Ulster Gaelic.[2]
- Were you ever at the feis at Corkadoragha, sir? said the Old-Grey-Fellow.
- I was na! said he, but I was carousing in Scotland.
- I thought, said I, that I saw you with the crowd of fellows that were gathered at the gate of the feis-field.
- I was na with thon crowd that were at the gate, Captain! said he.

~ Did you ever read *Séadna*?[3] said the Old-Fellow sincerely.

We continued conversing lightly and courteously together for a long while, discussing the affairs of the day and talking of the hard times. I gathered quite an amount of information about the Rosses from the other two during the conversation and also about the bad circumstances of the people there; all were barefoot and without means. Some were always in difficulty, others carousing in Scotland. In each cabin there was: (i) one man at least, called the 'Gambler', a rakish individual, who spent much of his life carousing in Scotland, playing cards and billiards, smoking tobacco and drinking spirits in taverns; (ii) a worn, old man who spent the time in the chimney-corner bed and who arose at the time of night-visiting to shove his two hooves into the ashes, clear his throat, redden his pipe and tell stories about the bad times; (iii) a comely lassie called Nuala or Babby or Mabel or Rosie for whom men came at the dead of every night with a five-noggin bottle and one of them seeking to espouse her. One knows not why but that is how it was. He who thinks that I speak untruly, let him read the good books, or the *guid buiks*.

At last we reached the Rosses and when we did, we had walked quite a portion of the earth's crust. Of course, it is a happy countryside even if it is hungry. For the first time since birth, I saw a countryside which was not drenched by the flowing of the rain. In every direction, the variegated colours of the firmament pleased the eye. A soft sweet breeze followed at our heels and helped us while we walked. High up in the skies there was a yellow lamp known as the sun, shedding heat and light down upon us. Far away there were tall blue stacks of mountains standing east and west and watching us. A nimble stream accompanied the main road; it was hidden in the bottom of the ditch but we knew of its presence because of the soft murmuring it bestowed on our ears. At both sides was a brown-black bog, speckled with rocks. I had no fault to find with the Rosses nor with any one of them. One Ross was as delightful as the other.

With regard to hunting, the Old-Grey-Fellow had commenced this before I noticed that the appearance of the countryside suggested that it was huntable or that the Old-Fellow was on the trail. He leaped suddenly over the fence. I followed him. Before us in a little field stood a strong stone-built house. In the twinkling of an eye the Old-Fellow had opened a window and had disappeared out of sight into the building. I stood for a moment pondering the wonders of life and then, as I was about to follow him through the window, he came out as precipitately.

- There was always good hunting in that house, said he to me. He opened his hand and what might one imagine was there but five shillings in silver, a fine elegant lady's necklace and a small golden ring. He placed these objects in some inside pocket with satisfaction and hurried me away with him onwards.

- 'Tis the schoolmaster, O'Beenassa, that owns that house, said he, and it's seldom I went off empty from it.

- If that's the way, sir, said I honestly, isn't it the unusual world that's there today and isn't the kind of hunting we're doing now very irregular?

- If that's the way, said the shrewd creature, 'tis time!

Having reached another slate-roofed house, the Old-Fellow entered it and returned after a time with a full fist of red money that he found in a cup on the dresser; in another house he stole a silver spoon; in yet another house he took such a quantity of food that it replaced our lost energy after the perambulations and difficulties of the day.

- Is it the way, said I finally, that there's no one alive in this countryside or is it that they're all cleared out from us to

America? Whatever way things are in this part of the world, all the houses are empty and everyone away from home.

- 'Tis clear, wee little son, said the Old-Fellow, that you haven't read the good books. 'Tis now the evening and according to literary fate, there's a storm down on the sea-shore, the fishermen are in difficulties on the water, the people are gathered on the strand, the women are crying and one poor mother is screaming: Who'll save my Mickey? That's the way the Gaels always had it with the coming of night in the Rosses.

- It's unbelievable, said I, the world that's there today.

And sure enough, having hunted and thieved from house to house, we came at last to a high hill from which we had a view of the edge of the ocean westwards where the big white-foamed waves were coming ashore. On the summit of the hill the weather was mild but it was evident from the angry appearance of the sea that the people below were in a storm of wind, and that the situation of the fisherman who was at sea could be unpleasant. I could not see the women on the strand weeping because of the distance between us but, doubtless, they were there.

We sat on a rock, I and the Old-Grey-Fellow, until we had rested. The pockets and clothes of the Old-Fellow were crammed as a result of his thieving, not to mention the valuable articles he had beneath his armpit and in his hand. He certainly had had an excellent bag that day and our visit was hardly of benefit to the people of the Rosses. The Old-Fellow requested me to carry some of the loot for him.

- We'll go now, said he, to the cabin of my friend, Ferdinand O'Roonassa, in Killeagh where I'll put down the night and you can move off home after having spuds and new milk for yourself. I'll get a little cart from Ferdinand and I'll be home tomorrow with all I've taken today, thanks to the hunting.

- Very well, sir, said I.

We went. Ferdinand lived in a little house in the corner of the glen as you journey westwards along the road. We received a great Gaelic welcome there. Ferdinand was an old worn man and only his daughter, Mabel, lived with him (a small, well-made, comely girl) and an old woman (it is unknown whether she was his wife or his mother) who was dying for twenty years in the bed in the chimney-corner and who was still on this side of the Great Contest. She had a son named Mickey (his nickname was the *Gambler*) but he was carousing yonder in Scotland.

The Old-Fellow's goods were concealed—it was evident that everyone had experience in this line of business—and then we all sat down to potatoes. When dietary business had been terminated, the Old-Grey-Fellow remarked to Ferdinand that I was a young person, lacking much knowledge of the world and that I never heard a real shanachee recounting real folklore in the old Gaelic manner.

- Therefore, Ferdinand, said he, you should tell us a story, please.

- Sure, I'd tell ye a story gladly, said Ferdinand, only that it isn't proper for a shanachee to talk in a house at night-visiting without settling himself down comfortably by the fire and putting his two hooves into the ashes; but I'm far off from the fire where I'm sitting and the pains won't let me get up and push my chair to the hob. 'Twas that misfortunate pair, the Sea-cat and the Peerkus, that gave me the same pains, death-tying to the two of them!

- Don't mind it, said the Old-Grey-Fellow, I'll pull up your chair and yourself as well.

No sooner was that said than it was done. The shanachee, O'Roonassa, was placed at the warm side of the fire and we all congregated about, heating ourselves, although the evening was not at all cold. I looked curiously at the shanachee. He settled his body luxuriantly in the chair, fixed his backside carefully beneath him, shoved his two hooves into the ashes, reddened his pipe and, when he was at his ease, he cleared his windpipe and began to spew discourse upon us.

- I did na know and I a little child in the ashes, said he, and our Pats or Mickileen or curly Nora of Big Nelly of young Peter did na know either, why he was called the Captain. However, the signs were on him that he spent a good bit of his life on the sea. It looked as if he liked his own company the best because he lived in a little lime-white house in the corner of the glen on the right-hand side as you go the road eastwards and begor, 'twas seldom the people of the place laid an eye on him. There was a far-off lonesome look about him and 'tis often I heard it said that there was some big shameful mark on his life. 'Twas said that he spent a good bit of his life carousing in Scotland, that he drank more than water and buttermilk when he was young and that 'twasn't the good thing he always did and he boozed, because he was a cross prickly fellow who never tried to tame the flood-tides of anger that come over everyone sometimes. Apart from that, he was a pleasant polite fellow to anyone who took to him, or that's what I heard. Many's the story and the tale of a story they had about him. They said he was a priest in Scotland, that he went a few steps out of the way and was put out of the Church. Other people said that he killed a man in a pub when he was young and came to the Rosses when on the run. Everyone had his own story.

Well, the Night of the Big Wind came. A heavy sea arose and, as usual, the fishermen were in difficulties in the mouth of the harbour, trying to come ashore. The wives and the women were standing, watching in torment the poor men on the shelf of rock, their boat broken in the water, and terrible breakers without number threatening them every minute with drowning, running in from the western dark of night and throwing great hanks of seaweed on the black brow of the rocks. Every great murderous wave drenched the watchers on the strand; they were wet to the marrow from the foam of the sea. A mother's shout arose above the scream of the wind: Oh! oh! who will save my Paddy?

Neither I nor Pats nor Mickileen nor young Peter's big Nelly's curly Nora expected the answer she got to this. There was a movement behind the people and forward came the Captain with a jump. He threw off his coat and was in the sea before sense could be talked to him. Ochone! said the people, another good man lost!

Well, there were struggle and effort and bad work and life and death that night in the sea; but to make a hard story easy, the Captain succeeded in reaching the rock, tying the two that were out there to the rope he had around him and, God save us all! the three of them were pulled safely ashore. It seems that the Captain damaged himself that night because he was found dead the next day.

'Twas in the wake-house I heard the full story.

When he was young and carousing in Scotland, the Captain killed a brother of one of the men on the rock and the sister of the other. He spent twenty years in jail yonder before he returned to settle down alone in the little house in the corner of the glen. Whatever sin was on his soul was cleaned off that night when he did the bold deed on the rock and made up fully for everything before he died. 'Tis amazing how fate drives us in this life from the bad act to the good one and back again. Doubtless, it was the Sea-cat that drove the Captain to the killing of the first two and another power put it in his power to bring the other two safe from the sentence of death. There are many things that we don't understand and will never understand.

The shanachee had come to the end and the Old-Fellow and myself thanked him liberally for this fine story which he had related.

Darkness was falling over the world by this time and I considered it time for me to set my foot on the long road ahead of me to Corkadoragha. As I was about to bid farewell, a polite and truly Gaelic knock came to the door and two men, whom I did not know, entered. Little was said before I understood that one of them had pledge of word and hand with curly-headed Mabel who was now slumbering in the end of the house and that they had a five-noggin bottle to complete the bargain and wish it success. I fondly bade farewell to Ferdinand and the Old-Grey-Fellow and went out under the nocturnal skies.

It was now dark in the Rosses but, I thought, the appearance of the world was somehow changed. I was outside for a while before I understood what was unusual around me. The ground was dry and no downpour came upon me. It was evident that the Rosses and Corkadoragha were dissimilar because no night came in the latter without showers of rain out of the skies pouring upon us. The night here was eerie and unnatural but, doubtless it had its own charm.

The Old-Fellow had already described the route to Corkadoragha to me and I set off vigorously. The stars lighted me, the ground beneath my feet was level and the cold condiment of the nocturnal wind sharpened my appetite for potatoes. We would have a high life for three months as a result of the thieving performed by my friend that day. I struck up a little whistling tune as I walked. I had a five-mile walk along by the sea, then inland towards the east, led by the whims of the by-roads. The crooning of the ocean remained in my ears for an hour with the salt smell of the seaweed swarming into my nose; nevertheless, I was travelling through maritime fields out of sight of the ocean. As I was about to part company with the sea, the path led me to a cliff-top and I stood for a while to look. There was a large sandy strand below; white where the quiet wavelets were

♣ *Then, the dull sheen in the sky increased slightly and I saw that a great strong hairy object was in my company that night, grey-haired and with prickly red eyes, staring at me angrily. The darkness had now become rotten with its breath, causing my health to forsake me at full speed.*

coming calmly ashore; rough and troubled near me at the foot of the cliff; filled with broken rocks which were hirsute with the herbs of the sea and bright with little water-pools which shone in the twilight and were awaiting patiently the full of the tide. Everything was so calm and peaceful that I sat down to enjoy the occasion where I was and to allow the fatigue to escape from my bones.

I should not say that I did not snooze a little but suddenly there was a great explosion in the midst of the stillness and I was again fully awake and on my guard, of course. Whatever demon or person was about, I thought that it was two hundred yards or thereabouts on my left-hand side and within the rugged area in the shade of the cliff and concealed where no eye could see it. I never heard such a peculiar, unrecognisable sound. On one hand, it was firm like one stone falling upon the other; on the other, it resembled a fat cow falling into a water-filled bog-hole. I remained motionless, listening, with my heart full of terror. There was now no sound there except what came softly from the water on the beach below. There was, however, another thing which I felt. The air was now putrid with an ancient smell of putridity which set the skin of my nose humming and dancing. Fear and melancholy and disgust came over me. The noise and that smell were connected! A strong desire came upon me to be at home safe and in the end of the house resting among the pigs. Loneliness came on me; I was alone in that place and the unknown evil thing had encountered me.

I do not know whether I was inquisitive or bold at that moment but a strong desire possessed me to investigate what was ahead and to ascertain whether there was any earthly explanation for the sound and smell which I had perceived. I arose and went west, east and then north, making no halt until I was standing below on the sand of the beach. The soft damp sand was beneath my feet. I walked carefully towards the location of the sound. The evil smell was now really strong and worsening with each footstep I took on my way. In spite of it, I advanced, praying that my courage should not fail me. A cloud had covered the stars and, for a while, the appearance of the land by the sea was not easily visible. Suddenly my eye comprehended one shadow which was blacker than the others which were at the foot of the cliff and the evil smell now assailed me in such a manner as to upset my stomach. I halted there to collect my wits and to grasp my courage. Before I had the opportunity, neverthe-less, to do either of these two things, the black object moved from where it was. Despite the great terror which captured me at that moment, my eyes observed every detail clearly before them. A large quadruped had arisen and was now standing in the midst of the rocks, spewing showers of putrid stench around it. At first I thought that an exceedingly bulky seal stood before me but later the four feet denied this. Then, the dull sheen in the sky increased slightly and I saw that a great strong hairy object was in my company that night, grey-haired and with prickly red eyes, staring at me angrily. The darkness had now become rotten with its breath, causing my health to forsake me at full speed. Suddenly there came from the evil thing a trembling and a snorting and I noticed that it was determined to attack me and, perhaps, to eat me. No word of Gaelic which I have ever heard can describe the terror which took hold of me. A fit of trembling oppressed my limbs from the crown of my head to the soles of my feet; my heart missed every other beat and the perspiration poured thickly from me. I thought at that stage that my career on the green soil of Ireland would be short. I never had such an unhealthy position as I had that night by the great ocean. The bitter lean fear, the small smooth cowardly fear, came suddenly upon me. Within me arose a storm of blood, a well of sweat and excessive fuss of mind. Another bark issued from the grey object yonder. At the same time a ghostly movement came in my feet, an unearthly movement which carried my body swiftly and with the lightness of wind over the rough land where I was. The evil thing was pursuing me. Coughing and a rotten stench were behind me, chasing and moving me over the Paradise of Ireland.

By the time I had once more regained perception and my comprehension of life, I had travelled a long distance. No longer did I have the great sea of seaweed and sand under my eyes and the evil spirit was no longer at my heels. I was safe from that nameless demon. I was neither injured nor eaten but, weary though I was, I did not desist from vehement flight until I was safe at home in Corkadoragha.

The following day the Old-Grey-Fellow returned to us with his hunting-bag. We welcomed him tenderly and we all sat down to potatoes. When everybody within the house, both porcine and human, was replenished with potatoes, I took the Old-Fellow aside and whispered in his ear. I stated that my health was not too good after the events of the preceding night.

- Is it boozing you were at, oh young little son, he said, or was it night-hunting?

- In truth, no sir! I replied, but a great thing on legs was chasing me. I don't know any word of Gaelic for it but it was not to my good, without a doubt. I don't know how I managed to escape from it but I'm here today and it's a great victory for me. 'Twould be a shameful thing if I was lost from this life and I in the flower of my youth because my likes will not be there again.

- Were you in Donegal at that time, my soul? said he.

- I was.

A ruminative cloud gathered over the face of the Old-Grey-Fellow.

- Could you put down on paper, said he, the shape and appearance of this savage thing for me?

The memory of the previous night was so firmly fixed in my mind that I made little delay in drawing an image of the creature when I had procured paper. It was thus:

The Old-Fellow looked closely at the picture* and a shadow crept over his visage.

- If that's how it is, son, said he fearfully, it's good news that you're alive today and in your health among us. What you met last night was the Sea-cat! The Sea-cat!!

The blood drained from my face when I heard that evil name being mentioned by the Old-Fellow.

- It seems, said he, that he was after coming out of the sea to carry out some mischievous work in the Rosses because he had often been in that area in the past, attacking the paupers and scattering death and ill-luck liberally among them. His name is always in the people's mouths there.

- The Sea-cat . . . ? said I. My feet were not too staunch beneath me while I stood there.

- The same cat.

- Is it the way, said I weakly, that no one else saw the Sea-cat before this?

- 'Tis my idea that they did, said he slowly, but no account of it was got from them. They did not live!

There was a little cessation of conversation between us.

- I'll go to the rushes, said I, and let you take to the pipe!

* The good reader will kindly notice the close resemblance between the Sea-cat, as delineated by O'Coonassa, and the pleasant little land which is our own. Many things in life are unintelligible to us but it is not without importance that the Sea-cat and Ireland bear the same shape and that both have all the same bad destiny, hard times and ill-luck attending on them which have come upon us.

Chapter 6

WHEN I HAD become a man (but was neither healthy nor virile) I thought one day that it was otherwise with me than it was with those in Corkadoragha who were my contemporaries and had grown up in my company. They were married and had numerous children. Doubtless, some of these were going to school at this time and being christened Jams O'Donnell by the master. I had no wife and it seemed to me that no one had a whit of respect for me as a result. At that stage I did not know the basic facts of life or anything else. I thought that babies fell out of the skies and that those who desired them needed only to have good luck and a fine spacious field. Nevertheless, I had a small suspicion that things were not thus. There were folks—old crippled persons—with large farms of land who were child-less, while other people who lacked land enough to support a hen but who had a house filled with little folks. I considered it a reasonable thing to lay this question before the Old-Grey-Fellow.

- Why and wherefore, sir, said I to him one day, am I not married?

- Whoever is patient, said he, is satisfied.

We said no more at that time but I pondered the matter for a month at my ease while stretched in the rushes at the end of the house. I noticed that men married women and women married men always. Although I often heard Martin O'Bannassa describe me as a poor creature when he was in my mother's company, I was of the opinion that many a woman would accept me willingly.

One day, when I was on the road, I met a lady from Upper Corkadoragha. She saluted me quietly and I addressed to her some few words.

- Lady, said I, I'm grown to man's age and you see I've got no family. Is there any chance, oh sprightly honest lady, that you'd marry me?

I received neither blessing nor kind reply but away she went along the road with all her might, swearing aloud. By the time that the nocturnal waters were descending, a tall robust black-haired man came to my mother inquiring about me. He held a blackthorn stick in his grasp and had a frown of great anger on him. My mother sensed that his plans did not include good deeds and sweet words where I was concerned and she said that I was absent from home and she expected me to return. It happened that I was at this moment in the position normal for me, *i.e.* resting in the rushes at the end of the house. The black-haired man departed from us but he uttered many foul words and unblessed epithets when he did so. His visit put terror into my heart because I realised that his visit had some connection with the lady whom I had met on the road.

After pondering the matter for another year, I approached the Old-Fellow once more.

- Honest fellow! said I, I'm two years waiting now without

a wife and I don't think I'll ever do any good without one. I'm afraid the neighbours are mocking me. Do you think is there any help for the fix I'm in or will I be all alone until the day of my death and everlasting burial?

- Boy! said the Old-Fellow, 'twould be necessary for you to know some girl.

- If that's the way, I replied, where do you think the best girls are to be got?

- In the Rosses, without a doubt!

The Sea-cat entered my mind and I became a little worried. However, there is little use denying the truth and I trusted the Old-Fellow.

- If 'tis that way, said I in a bold voice, I'll go to the Rosses tomorrow to get a woman.

The Old-Fellow was dissatisfied with this kind of thing and endeavoured for a while to coax me from the marriage-fever that had come upon me but, of course, I had no desire to break the resolution which was fixed for a year in my mind. He yielded finally and informed my mother of the news.

- Wisha! said she, the poor creature!

- If he manages to get a woman out of the Rosses, said the Old-Grey-Fellow, how do we know but that she'll have a dowry? Wouldn't the likes of that be a great help to us at present in this house when the spuds are nearly finished and the last drop reached in the end of the bottle with us?

- I wouldn't say that you haven't the truth of it! said my mother.

They decided at last to yield completely to me. The Old-Fellow said that he was acquainted with a man in Gweedore who had a nice curly-headed daughter who was, as yet, unmarried although the young men from the two sandbanks were all about her, frenzied with eagerness to marry. Her father was named Jams O'Donnell and Mabel was the maiden's name. I said that I would be satisfied to accept her.

The following day the Old-Fellow put a five-noggin bottle in his pocket and both of us set out in the direction of Gweedore. In the middle of the afternoon we reached that townland after a good walk while the daylight was still in the heavens. Suddenly the Old-Fellow halted and sat down by the roadside.

- Are we yet near the habitation and enduring home of the gentleman, Jams O'Donnell? asked I softly and quietly, querying the Old-Fellow.

- We are! said he. There is his house over yonder.

- Fair enough, said I. Come on till we settle the deal and get our evening spuds. There's a sharp hunger on my hunger.

- Little son! said the Old-Fellow sorrowfully, I'm afraid that you don't understand the world. 'Tis said in the good books that describe the affairs of the Gaelic paupers that it's in the middle of the night that two men come visiting if they have a five-noggin bottle and are looking for a woman. Therefore we must sit here until the middle of the night comes.

- But 'twill be wet tonight. The skies above are full.

- Never mind! There's no use for us trying to escape from fate, oh bosom friend!

We did not succeed in escaping that night either from fate or the rain. We were drenched into the skin and to the bones. When we reached Jams O'Donnell's floor finally, we were completely saturated, water running from us freely, wetting both Jams and his house as well as every thing and living creature present. We quenched the fire and it had to be rekindled nine times.

Mabel was in bed (or had gone to her bed) but there is no necessity for me to describe the stupid conversation carried on by the Old-Fellow and Jams when they were discussing the question of the match. All the talk is available in the books

♣ 'Tis said in the good books that describe the affairs of the Gaelic paupers that it's in the middle of the night that two men come visiting if they have a five-noggin bottle and are looking for a woman.

which I have mentioned previously. When we left Jams at the bright dawn of day, the girl was betrothed to me and the Old-Fellow was drunk. We reached Corkadoragha at the midhour of day and were well satisfied with the night's business.

I need hardly remark that there were revelry and high frolics in this townland when my wedding-day came. The neighbours arrived to congratulate me. The Old-Fellow had, by this time, drunk the dowry-money which he had procured and there was not a good drop in the house to offer to the neighbours. When they realised that matters were thus, gloom and ill-humour took hold of them. Threatening whispers were heard from the men occasionally and the women set themselves to devouring all our potatoes and drinking all our butter-milk so as to inflict a three-month's scarcity upon us. A species of terror came upon the Old-Fellow when he saw how matters stood with the company. He whispered privily in my ear.

- Fellow! said he, if this gang doesn't get spirits and tobacco from us, I'm afraid one of our pigs will be stolen from us this night.

- All the pigs and my wife will be stolen as well, sir, I replied.

Mabel was in the end of the house at this juncture with my mother on top of her. The poor girl was trying to escape back to her father's house and my mother endeavouring to make her see reason and informing her that it is compulsory to submit to Gaelic fate. There was great weeping and tumult that night in our house.

It was Martin O'Bannassa himself who rescued us. When everything was truly in a bad state, he walked in carrying a small barrel of true water under his armpit. He quietly presented me with the barrel and congratulated me courteously on my marriage. When the company inside realised that the door of hospitality was finally opened, they wished to be merry and good-humoured and commenced to drink, dance and make music with all their might. After some time, they made a racket which shook the walls of the house, dismaying and terrorising the pigs. The woman in the end of the house was given a full cup of that fiery water—despite the fact that she had no stomach for it—and before long she ceased her struggling and fell into a drunken slumber in the rushes. According as the men drank their fill, they lost the inherited good manners and good habits they had. By the time midnight had come, blood was being spilled liberally and there were a few men in the company without a stitch of clothing about them. At three in the morning, two men died after a bout of fighting which arose in the end of the house— poor Gaelic paupers without guile who had no experience of the lightning-water in Martin's barrel. As for the Old-Fellow, he almost faced eternity together with the other two. He was not in the fight and no blow was struck on him but during the dancing he sat in a place near the barrel. I considered that it was a good thing that my wife lost her senses and was not aware of the conduct of that wedding-feast. There was no sweet sound there and any hand which was raised did not accomplish a good deed.

Yes! when I had been married a month or so, contention and angry speech arose between my wife and my mother. The situation worsened daily and at last the Old-Fellow advised us to clear out of the house altogether and to settle down in another place because, said he, it has always been thus with every newly-wed couple. It was neither right nor proper, said he, that two women should live under the same roof. It was clear to me that the trouble between them was annoy- ing him and disturbing his night's sleep. We adapted for our habitation the old hut which had been formerly built for the animals. When that was accomplished, and we had installed the beds of rushes, I and my wife left the other house together with two pigs and a few small household effects to begin life in the new domicile. Mabel was skilled in potato-boiling and we lived together peacefully for a year, both of us companionable in the end of the house. Often the Old-Grey-Fellow came in to converse with us in the afternoon.

Yes! life is extraordinary. One time when I returned from Galway in the black of night, what do you think I noticed but that we had acquired a new piglet in the end of the house. My wife was sleeping while the tiny little bright-skinned thing was squealing in the centre of the house. I took it carefully and allowed it to drop from my hand with amazement when I realised precisely what I had. It had a small bald head, a face as large as a duck-egg and legs like my own. I had a baby-child. Need I say that the sudden raising of my heart was both joyous and indescribable? We had a young male child! I felt importance and superiority filling my heart and substance coming in my body!

I left the kitten gently down alongside his mother and rushed out to the Old-Fellow, holding the bottle of spirits which I had kept hidden for a year. We drank a glass and yet another glass together in the darkness and then we drank the health of the young son. After some time, when some of the neighbours heard the shouting and the inebriated commotion that we caused, they knew that true water was available for nothing and they arose from their rushy beds and congregated in to keep us company. We had a great night until morning. We decided to name the young man Leonard O'Coonassa.

Alas! happiness is not lasting and neither is joy for any Gaelic pauper because he does not escape for long the scourging of fate. One day, while playing on the sward in front of the door with Leonardo when he was a year and a day old, I noticed some indisposition come suddenly upon him and that he was not far from eternity. His little face was grey and a destructive cough attacked his throat. I grew terrified when I could not calm the creature. I left him down on the grass and ran in to find my wife. What do you think but that I found her stretched out, cold in death on the rushes, her mouth wide open while the pigs snorted around her. When I reached Leonardo again in place I had left him, he was also lifeless. He had returned whence he had come.

Here then, reader, is some evidence for you of the life of the Gaelic paupers in Corkadoragha and an account of the fate which awaits them from their first day. After great merriment comes sorrow and good weather never remains for ever.

Chapter 7

THERE WAS a man in this townland at one time and he was named Sitric O'Sanassa. He had the best hunting, a generous heart and every other good quality which earn praise and respect at all times. But alas! there was another report abroad concerning him which was neither good nor fortunate. He possessed the very best poverty, hunger and distress also. He was generous and open-handed and he never possessed the smallest object which he did not share with the neighbours; nevertheless, I can never remember him during my time possessing the least thing, even the quantity of little potatoes needful to keep body and soul joined together. In Corkadoragha, where every human being was sunk in poverty, we always regarded him as a recipient of alms and compassion. The gentlemen from Dublin who came in motors to inspect the paupers praised him for his Gaelic poverty and stated that they never saw anyone who appeared so truly Gaelic. One of the gentlemen broke a little bottle of water which Sitric had, because, said he, it spoiled the effect. There was no one in Ireland comparable to O'Sanassa in the excellence of his poverty; the amount of famine which was delineated in his person. He had neither pig nor cup nor any household goods. In the depths of winter I often saw him on the hillside fighting and competing with a stray dog, both contending for a narrow hard bone and the same snorting and angry barking issuing from them both. He had no cabin either, nor any acquaintance with shelter or kitchen heat. He had excavated a hole with his two hands in the middle of the countryside and over its mouth he had placed old sacks and branches of trees as well as any useful object that might provide shelter against the water which came down on the countryside every night. Strangers passing by thought that he was a badger in the earth when they perceived the heavy breathing which came from the recesses of the hole as well as the wild appearance of the habitation in general.

One day when I, the Old-Grey-Fellow and Martin O'Bannassa were sitting together on the brow of a hillock discussing the hard life and debating the poor lot which was now (and would always be) Ireland's, our conversation turned to our own folks at home and the potato scarcity and especially to Sitric O'Sanassa.

- I don't think, sirs, said Martin, that Sitric has got a spud for two days.

- Upon me soul, said the Old-Fellow, but you're truly right, and there's no health to be got from the rough grass that covers this hill.

- I saw the poor fellow yesterday, said I, and he outside drinking the rainwater.

- 'Tis a tasty drop if 'tisn't nourishing, said the Old-Fellow. If the Gaels could get food out of the sky's rain, I don't think there would be a thin belly in all this area.

- If 'tis my opinion the nice company wants, said Martin, I'd say that the same poor harmless man is not far off from eternity. Whoever is without a spud for long is unhealthy.

- Oh people of the sweet words, said I earnestly, unless my eyes are astray, Sitric is now coming out of his cave.

Down on the level land Sitric was standing and gazing about him, a tall spear of a man who was so thin with hunger that one's eye might fail to notice him if he were standing laterally towards one. He appeared both gay and foolish, lacking any proper control over his feet because of the inebriation caused to him by the morning air. Having stood for a while, he collapsed in a weakness on the bog.

- There's not much standing, said the Old-Grey-Fellow, in anyone who's long without a spud.

- 'Tis the truth you've told there, friend, said Martin, and that truth is true.

- For fear, oh respectable great ones, said I, that he is going from us at the present moment and taking a step in the way of all truth, I judge that it would be a good thing for us to speak with him at least, if only to prosper him on his course.

They agreed with me and down we went until we were in the same place as the infirm one. He stirred when he perceived the footsteps about him and saluted us in a low voice but courteously and kindly. Frankly, he was in a low state at this time. His breath was escaping feebly from him and, as to the red blood within him, there was no evidence of its presence to be seen on any part of his skin.

- Is it long since you ate a bite of food, Sitric, oh friend of friends? inquired Martin genially.

- I didn't taste a spud for a week, replied Sitric to him, and it's a month since I tasted a bit of fish. All that's laid before me at mealtime is hunger itself and I don't even get salt with that. I ate a scrap of turf last night and I wouldn't say that this black feeding agreed too well with my belly, God save us all! I was empty last night but now, anyway, my belly is full of pains. Isn't it slowly, friends, that death comes to him who desires it?

♣ *There was no one in Ireland comparable to O'Sanassa in the excellence of his poverty; the amount of famine which was delineated in his person. He had neither pig nor cup nor any household goods. In the depths of winter I often saw him on the hillside fighting and competing with a stray dog, both contending for a narrow hard bone and the same snorting and angry barking issuing from them both.*

- Woe to him who eats the bog! said the Old-Fellow. There is no health in the turf but, of course, how do we know but that we'll have the bogs and hills yet for food, God save the hearers!

Sitric moved out of the position he was in and rolled over on his back on the ground with his bloodshot eyes staring at us.

- Worthy people, said he, would ye carry me to the seaside and throw me into the sea? There's not the weight of a rabbit in me and 'twould be a small deed for well-fed sound men to throw me over a cliff.

- There's no fear for you, my soul! said Martin sadly, because there'll be a spud of mine for you while we've pigs at home and a pot boiling for them. You there, said he to me, over with you and get a big spud from the pigs' pot in my own wee cabin.

I set off with a will and did not halt until I had procured the biggest potato in the pot and had brought it back to the place of famine. The man on the ground devoured the potato greedily and when he had swallowed the meal, I noticed that he had recovered remarkably from his ill-health. He sat up.

- That was the tasty eating and I'm full up of thanks, said he, but you see I'm not so pleased to be begging from ye or to be leaving the pigs short. I'll be for ever without a house and the sooner I'm thrown into the sea, the sooner ye'll all be easy. I want to be under the water and never come up again . . .

- I never heard, said the Old-Fellow, that anyone was ever at ease who went off to sea without a boat under him!

- . . . Bad as the salt-sea is, replied Sitric, 'twould be easy on the fellow who lives in this dirty hole and the downpour on top of his head every night and with nothing in front of him but constant muck, the wet and raw famine . . .

- Don't forget, said I, that you're a Gael and that it isn't happiness that's in store for you!

- ... and the distress and the hardship and ill-luck ... said Sitric.

- 'Tisn't natural to have the showers down on top of us always, said the Old-Fellow, without a spot of sunlight between them an odd time.

- ... and the rotten badgers and the Sea-cat and the brown sea-mice that come on top of my head every night ... said Sitric.

- How do we know, said Martin, but that the sun will reach Corkadoragha yet?

- ... and for ever to the devil's end is misery, trouble and exhaustion; weather, frost, snow, thunder and lightning; the spite of the earth down every night out of the skies ...

- O'Sanassa will have another day![1] said I, like a false prophet.

- ... and the fleas! said Sitric.

It was apparent that he was ill-humoured, badly situated, in bad shape and in a bad way. I had never heard him swearing nor complaining previously. This type of thing was not correct nor Gaelic and we made an attempt to quieten him and cheer him up, lest he might go into the ocean unknown to us later. Martin O'Bannassa uttered the timely word.

- I was in Dingle yesterday, said he, and I was talking to a man from the Great Blasket. He said that seals were plentiful on Irish Mickelaun and that the islanders were intending to kill a few head of them. The oil is valuable and the meat tastes nice.

- There's danger in that work, friend! said I.

I did not relish very much any proposition to confront and, perhaps, handle these fellows. It occurred to me that one might quite easily garner death or injury while tackling this business.

- I thought, said Martin, that 'twould be a good thing for us to bring off a couple of them from the Rock to Corkadoragha. If we had oil, the darkness wouldn't be so heavy.

- I'd rather, said I, to be alive in the darkness than dead in much light.

I noticed the Old-Fellow frown, a sign that within his skull great labour was in progress. Finally he spoke:

- Look here, Sitric, said he, if you had a whole seal for yourself and he salted in your house, there would be no danger of famine for you in three months and you wouldn't be looking for begged spuds. I'd say we should *all* go into the sea, kill the seals in the holes and bring them home with us.

- There's sense in that saying, sweet fellow, said Sitric, but I couldn't fight the smallest seal that was ever on a sea-rock because I can't stand on my feet at the present.

- Don't mind that, son, said Martin, I'll send you a boy tonight with two more spuds and tomorrow we'll all set out on the waves when you'll have strength and vigour in you.

The matter was left thus. Despite the fact that the Old-Fellow said that we were *all* going on the waves, I left the bed very early on the following morning and, when I had consumed a moiety of potato, I faced for the hill. I had never been at sea and had no appetite for that kind of business and it appeared that, as long as I knew what would benefit me, I would never go to slay seals in that region under the sea which is their natural habitat. I considered that the best health on that day was obtainable on the hillsides. I had a couple of cold potatoes as sustenance and spent the whole day quietly sitting on my backside underneath the rain, pretending to be hunting. When it was light, I noticed the Old-Grey-Fellow, Martin O'Bannassa and Sitric O'Sanassa meeting and departing seawards with pikes, ropes, knives and other useful objects on their shoulders.

During the day, showers of rain came upon me and I was soaked and exhausted, of course, when I reached the house at nightfall. I went eagerly to the potatoes and when I had swallowed them, inquired about those who were abroad. My mother listened to the gale which assailed the house and when she relaxed, I noticed that she was worried.

- I don't think, said she, that this group will return safely tonight because they were never before at sea. Woe to whoever drew the journey on them!

- The rowing and swimming that's to be found on the hill, said I, is far nicer!

I brought in the pigs and we all went to the rush-beds. At this time the rain was pelting roughly on the house; great voices of thunder were shouting in the heights of the heavens; flashes of lightning which one might not see east or west were cleaving the darkness; dashes of the very brine were bursting over the window-glass although ten miles of road separated the house from the edge of the sea-shore. On a night such as this, of course, the ones who were out would not be worried about seals but rather endeavouring to learn the sailor's skill in one single effort with the object of reaching land safely. I also remembered that I would be the head of the house if it happened that the Old-Fellow failed to return from his sea-journey.

After all, things are not what they appear to be, in Corkadoragha at any rate. By the time that daylight had arrived and tranquillity had returned to the weather, the Old-Fellow and Martin O'Bannassa came in the door, both extremely exhausted and wet to the marrow; yet they called loudly for potatoes. Great welcomes were given to them and the table was prepared for food.

- Where's the third man that was with ye on the journey? said I. Is Mister O'Sanassa here in the company of the blessed yonder?

- He's alive and in excellent health, said Martin, but he is still under the sea.

- Wisha, said I, that's good but I pledge you, word and hand, sir, that I don't understand your talk.

When they had become belly-swollen with abundance of potatoes, the two sailors explained the night's business to me and it was an amazing business without a word of a lie. It appears that the three borrowed a canoe in Dunquin and they went away to the Rock. By the time they had arrived at the seals' home, they noticed a large hole in the flank of a rock and tested it with an oar. The hole led under sea-level and there was a strong surge of water around it. None of the three in the canoe had any great desire to dive into this mysterious region and they remained as they were for a long while, their verbal exceeding their venatic labours. Finally the older pair blew such a gale of advice and speech into the ears of O'Sanassa that he agreed to bind a rope around his waist and jump down in one bound into the depths of the hole. He went and was given plenty of rope. The sea was becoming choppy by this time and the sky looked bad. O'Sanassa had promised to return to the surface when he had the opportunity to report on the lower regions to the pair who were dry. There was no account of him, nevertheless, and in the course of time, the tune of the wind did not show any improvement. They decided to draw in the rope and to pull the fellow below safely out of the water by force. They heaved mightily on the rope but did not succeed; it remained fast against the opening of the hole. While they were consulting together after ceasing to pull, what should you imagine but that they felt a stir in the rope; the one below informing them that he was not in eternity! By this time the wind and the rain were locked together, the canoe was at one stage high in the sky and at another at the bottom of the great sea and ocean. The Old-Fellow resolved to head eastwards towards land and leave the one below where he was, considering how long he had spoken about the lower regions! Martin, however, opposed this plan. It seemed to him that he would never see ground or land again because of the volume of sea-water and wind that were around him, above him and beneath him. He decided it might be shrewd to move down to where O'Sanassa was still alive. He donned the appearance of courage, bade adieu to the Old-Fellow and leaped into the sea. The Old-Fellow was alone for a long time, awaiting news from the pair below, probably, and both loneliness and fear came upon him. The tempest became more boisterous, neither the sky nor the sea nor the sandy wind distinguishable one from the other. It is not known whether the Old-Fellow headed down into the seals' hole or was blown out of the boat but, at all events, he moved down to the lower reaches of the sea. His head was injured and, unfortunately, his bones also on the spikes of rock when he entered the sea; there was a strong pull in the hole and he was swallowed without delay. When he had regained command of his senses again, he was stretched on a ledge of rock which stood clear and dry of the water, with daylight shining down upon him from a crevice high up and away from where he was. It happened that there was a bend in the cave; initially it went under the water and then curved upwards through the crag. Apparently there was a large spacious room there, a fine shore here and a trough of water yonder where all was serene after the tempest outside. When the Old-Fellow's eyes had been accustomed to the dim light of this place, he noticed O'Sanassa and O'Bannassa together, sitting by a dead seal, chewing the tasteless meat. He went towards them and greeted them.

- Where did ye get the black fellow? said he to Martin.
- There's a houseful of them in the bottom of the hole, both large and small, said Martin. Be seated at the table, mister!

That is how they were accommodated for the night. They rigged a lamp for oil which was squeezed out of the seal's liver and spent the time conversing about the hard life and the minimal nourishment which Gaels would ever have. By the time that morning had come, the Old-Fellow stated that it was unnatural for him to lack a potato for so long a period and that he had decided, therefore, to face up into the water and set out for home. Martin praised this speech but would you believe that Sitric stretched out a hand to them, bidding them farewell and a prosperous voyage.

- Upon me soul! said the Old-Fellow to Martin in amazement, and the devil sweep you!

Mr O'Sanassa then expounded his own view of the situation. Where he was, he had freedom from the inclement weather, the famine and the abuse of the world. Seals would constitute his company as well as his food. Sky-water dripped from the roof of the cave which would serve both as condiment and as wine against thirst. It did not appear that he would desert such a well-built comfortable abode after all he had experienced of the misery of Corkadoragha. That was definite, he declared.

- Everyone to his own counsel! said Martin, but I've no wish to live under the sea any longer.

They left him there and there he has been ever since then. At times since then he has been seen at high tide, wild and hirsute as a seal, vigorously providing fish with the community with whom he lodged. I often have heard the neighbours say that Mr O'Sanassa was a skilful fisherman because he had, by this time, grown into a tasty fish and that a whole winter's oil was within him. I do not think, of course, that anyone has had the courage to chase him. To this day he is buried alive and is satisfied, safe from hunger and rain over on the Rock.

Chapter 8

IN ONE WAY or another, life was passing us by and we were suffering misery, sometimes having a potato and at other times having nothing in our mouths but sweet words of Gaelic. As far as the weather in itself was concerned, things were becoming worse. It seemed to us that the rainfall was becoming more offensive with each succeeding year and an occasional pauper was drowned on the very mainland from the volume of water and celestial emesis which poured down upon us; a non-swimmer was none too secure in bed in these times. Great rivers flowed by the doorway and, if it be true that the potatoes were all swept from our fields, it is also a fact that fish were often available by the wayside as a nocturnal exchange. Those who reached their beds safely on dry land, by the morning found themselves submerged. At night people often perceived canoes from the Blaskets going by and the boatmen considered it a poor night's fishing which did not yield to them a pig or a piglet from Corkadoragha in their nets. It has been said that O'Sanassa swam over from the Rock one night to gaze again at his native countryside; but who knows whether the visitor was but a common seal. It need hardly be said that the local people became peevish at that time; hunger and misfortune assailed them and they were not dry for three months. Many of them set out for eternity gladly and those who remained in Corkadoragha lived on little goods and great littleness there. One day I put the matter to the Old-Fellow and I entered into conversation with him.

- Do you think, oh gentle person, said I, that we'll ever again be dry?

- I really don't know, oh mild one, said he, but if this rain goes on like this, 'tis my idea that the fingers and toes of the Gaelic paupers will be closed and have webs on them like the ducks from now on to give them a chance of moving through the water. This is no life for a human being, son!

- Are you certain that the Gaels are people? said I.

- They've that reputation anyway, little noble, said he, but no confirmation of it has ever been received. We're not horses nor hens; seals nor ghosts; and, in spite of all that, it's unbelievable that we're humans—but all that is only an opinion.

- Do you think, oh sublime ancient, said I, that there will ever be good conditions for the Gaels or will we have nothing for ever but hardship, famine, nocturnal rain and Sea-cattishness?

- We'll have it all, said he, and day-rain with it.

- If we do, I replied, it's my opinion that 'tis well for O'Sanassa over on the Rock. He won't be badly off while fish are in the sea for food and he'll have a sleeping-hole in the Rock on the day of storm.

- You may be sure that the seals have their own troubles, said the Old-Fellow. They're the worried unhappy fellows.

- Is it the way, said I, that the great bursts of rain were just as heavy before this as they are now in these times?

The Old-Grey-Fellow displayed a brown-toothed laugh, a sign that my question had but little sense in it.

- You may as well know, young quiet one, said he, that this rain is only a summer shower to the fellow who knows about the times that were there long ago. In my grandfather's time there were people that never felt dry ground or a healthy place for sleeping from birth till death and who never tasted anything but fish and sky-water. 'Twas fish we used have in the field that time. Whoever couldn't swim well, went off to heaven.

- Is that the way it was?

- But in that time I heard my father praising the good weather and saying it was fine and that there was nothing wrong with it compared with the sky-crucifying that people got and he a young fellow. The people that time thought that the time of the Deluge was after coming again.

- Did anyone live after the great waters of that time? said I.

- Only an occasional person lived. But the weather was so contrary ages before that again, that it is said that everyone in the countryside was drowned except a man named Maeldoon O'Poenassa.[1] The man was intelligent and shrewd enough to put together the first boat in this part of the country and to rig it, a job that benefited him. He went off, alive and safe, on the high tide and took all kinds of things left behind by the people who had said goodbye to this life —fine spuds, torn alive from the ground by the flood, small household effects, little drops of spirits and valuable pieces of gold that were put aside for ages. By the time that he escaped from Corkadoragha, he was rich and thoroughly satisfied with himself without a doubt, I promise you.

- And where did he go in the boat, darling fellow? said I, greatly interested in his talk. My friend pointed his wrinkled finger to the White Bens which were away from us north-eastwards.

- The middle one of these is called Hunger-stack, said he, because O'Poenassa succeeded in reaching the top of that peak. In these times it was like an island of the sea to a boatman and 'tis said that he was the only man who got to the top of the mountain; it was too steep and the way up was troublesome for a fellow depending on his feet.

- Did he ever come down?

- Never truly! The way that's too steep going up is the same coming down and whoever would go footing the path down from the top would be undertaking self-destruction and 'twould be eternity he'd reach instead of the level land. He landed from the boat on the peak and himself and the boat are there since—if the sign of their remains is to be noticed there now.

- It appears, therefore, blessed man, said I with great beneficient thoughts oozing from me at that time, that there are precious non-contemptible articles on the top of Hunger-stack until this day—golden pennies and every other thing which O'Poenassa snatched away with him on the day of the squall?

- They're there, said he, if what we have in Corkadoragha of storytelling-gems and next-door-folklore from our ancestors and ancients is true and believable.

- 'Tis sweet hearing what you've told, old man of the liberality, said I, and my thankfulness is thankful to you.

By the time that I had reached the rushes that night, I did not get a wink nor an ounce of sleep due to the multitude of thoughts which assailed me and lured me on the subject of Hunger-stack. With the keen mind's eye I saw the summit of the mountain, the ribs of the boat and the man's bones clearly and, near them in that lonely place, all the plundered fortune which O'Poenassa took away with him in the time of the Deluge. I thought that this was a great shame—paupers suffering from famine here and means of salvation yonder and no means of acquiring it at hand. I should say that at this point of time I formed the resolution of going to the summit of that mountain one day of my life whether I was dead or alive, big or small, belly-cheered or in the depths of hunger. I was of the opinion that one might be better off seeking death searching for the good life on Hunger-stack than suffering hard times for ever in Corkadoragha. It were better for a man to die on the mountain from celestial water than to live at home famished in the centre of the plain. I considered the matter for myself during the night and, in that half-bright time when the day was breaking in upon the blackness of night, I had decided everything in my mind. I would go to Hunger-stack one day. I would go to seek the money and if I returned home safely after all the difficulty, I would be henceforward exceedingly rich, bellyful, frequently inebriated.

Lest there be nothing on the summit but nourishment for myself, I decided to keep the resolution in my own mind firmly and strongly and neither to share it with the neighbours nor inform the Old-Fellow of it. I began then to observe the course of the bad weather, taking note of the ways of the tempest and the customs of the winds to discover whether there was any part of day or year more suitable than another for travelling to Hunger-stack. For a year, that is how things were and at the end of that time, I noticed that my labours were all in vain. In Corkadoragha the height of the wind and the strength of the rain were always similar, night and day without fail, in summer as in winter. It was a silly business to wait for the day of fine weather and, finally, I decided that it was time for me to set out on my course.

The shoulder of the mountain was so steep and my health so precarious that my little wretched back was capable of carrying only a light and slender load. I collected secretly what few things that were necessary—a bottle of water, a knife, a bag for the gold and a measure of potatoes.

I remember well the morning I started on my journey. The water was bursting out of the sky in such profusion that it terrified me and injured the crown of my head. At first I had not resolved to journey to the mountain that day but I considered that the country-folk were about to be drowned and that it appeared I would be safe if I succeeded even in climbing a few steps up the flank of the hill. Were it not for the heavy precipitation of that morning, it is to be feared that I would never have had the courage to forsake the little house where I was born and face the mountain of destiny; my ominous unknown objective.

It was dark. When I pulled my body out of the damp rushes, I grasped my travelling bundle which I had concealed in a hollow in the wall and I quietly moved out. The rain and the wild appearance of the infernal twilight struck fear and terror into my heart. I discovered the place where I judged the main road to be and I shuffled along, walking and half-walking, falling and half-falling, towards the mountain. A stream of water, which reached my knees, was coming strongly against me and certainly my movement at that time was not very good but consisted of constant stumbling and half-limping, at one time stretched in the watery muck, occasionally lifted from the earth by the spite of the wind and wrapped up in the rainy gale, unable to control my person. Doubtless, that morning I possessed Gaelic misery.

After all the difficulty, I was clearly advancing a little, because I felt the ground rising beneath me and causing me more hardship. Salty showers of perspiration bubbled down over my eyes to add to my other miseries and I thought my feet were bathed more by blood than water. But I was now set on my course and had no wish to yield to anything but death alone.

When I was fairly far up on the ridge of the hill, I noticed a flood of rivers of water bearing down upon me together with trees, large stones and small farms of land; to this day I am amazed how I failed to acquire a mortal fracture of the skull from this diabolical onrush. At times home-sickness came over me but nevertheless courage did not entirely fail me. With all my might I pressed onwards although I was often pressed backwards by a lump of the mountain hitting the crown of my head. I assure you that I spent that night-till-day working with my two feet and that labour was strenuous and sudorific.

When the puny semi-illumination which passes for day among us in Corkadoragha arrived, what an amazing sight was revealed to me! I found myself almost on the summit of the mountain, my colour alternating between red and blue because of the bloodshed and the nocturnal buffetings, while my body was stripped of the last scrap of cloth. The crown of my head almost touched the black-bellied fierce clouds and a great deluge of rain issued from them; a deluge so heavy that my hair was being plucked rapidly from me. In spite of every effort and stout endeavour on my part, I was drinking the very rain and became dangerously belly-swollen, something which did not improve my control of walking. Beneath me I noticed naught but mist and morning vapours. Above, I saw the mountain occasionally, while around me was nothing but rocks, filth and the continual moist gale. I moved on. It was an amazing place and very amazing also was the weather. I think its like will not be there again.

Without a doubt I was a long while on the summit before

I noticed the exact lie of the land. On the summit was a little flat plain, pools of water behind and yonder, yellow fretful rivers flowing between them and filling my ears with an unearthly mysterious humming. In places there were villages of leaning white rocks or a mesh of bottomless dark-mouthed holes where rapid waters were falling incessantly. Certainly the area did not have a normal appearance and, although Corkadoragha was bad, I should have praised it gladly at that hour.

I proceeded to visit and examine minutely the place by walking, falling and swimming in an endeavour to discover whether there was any trace of the boat or any account of Maeldoon O'Poenassa. Hunger was tickling my intestines and an indescribable fatigue filling my limbs with unhealthy drowsiness. However, since I knew that I was nigh to eternity and that I had little opportunity to better my lot, I continued sliding forwards and backwards erratically with my eye seeking eagerly for some human habitation while my throat sought to avoid swallowing an excessive quantity of rain. It was thus for a long while.

I do not know whether I allowed a large part of the day to slip by in sleep or in semi-consciousness, but if it were thus, it amazes me now that I ever awoke again. Be that as it may, it was apparent to me that the twilight of the night was coming on the day of morning and that the cold and strength of the tempest were increasing. By this time I had lost all my blood and was on the point of bowing to fate, lying willingly in the mud and setting my face towards heaven when I noticed a little light shining weakly far away from me, half-lost in the mist and the sheets of rain. A little start of joy stirred in my heart. Strength returned to my body and I set off cripple-footed but energetically towards the light, if it were really such. This, I thought, was all that lay between me and the mouth of perpetual eternity.

It really was a light that was issuing from a cave which ran between two rocks. The cave-mouth was narrow and slender but, of course, I was as thin as an oar from the misery, the hardship and the loss of blood of the previous day. I was inside and safe from the gale without delay; before me was the light and I approached it. I had had no experience of creeping in a stone cave but nevertheless my movement was nimble as I went towards the location of that flame within.

When I had reached the spot, I believed that I was not overly satisfied with the situation of the place, the company present or the business in hand. Within there was a cell or small room with space for four or five men; bare and rocky it was with water dripping from the walls. Great flames of fire arose from the stony floor and, in the background, a well of fresh water bubbled up animatedly, forming a stream which flowed towards me in the cave. However what almost took the sight from my eyes was an old person, half-sitting, half-lying by the flames and away from me, a species of chair beneath him and his appearance suggested that he was dead. A few unrecognisable rags were wrapped around him, the skin of his hand and face was like wrinkled brown leather and he had an appearance totally unnatural about him. His two eyes were closed, his black-toothed mouth was open and his head inclined feebly to one side. A fit of trembling seized me, stemming from both cold and fear. I had finally met Mael-doon O'Poenassa!

I recalled suddenly the resolution which led me to this place and, God save the hearers! no sooner did I remember the golden pennies than I held them in my grasp! They were scattered near at hand, here and there about the floor, thousands of them, together with golden rings, gems, pearls and heavy yellow chains. The leather satchel from which they had come was there and it was really fortunate that this was so because I was stark naked at this time and both packless and pocketless. My hands automatically collected the pennies and before long the bag held as much gold as I was capable of carrying. While engaged in this activity, I felt my heart recover and play a little musical tune.

I had no desire whatever to look towards the dead man and when the gold was collected, I proceeded to creep back through the cave. I had reached the opening with the terrifying voices of wind and rain assaulting my ears, when a luckless thought struck me with a thud.

If Maeldoon O'Poenassa were dead, who had lighted the fire and who tended it?

I do not know whether a fit of frenzy took hold of me at this time or whether I died temporarily from fear but what I did was to return back to the fellow who was within. I found him there exactly as I had left him. I moved timidly towards him, proceeding across the watery floor on feet, belly and hands. Suddenly one of my hands slipped and my head fell, causing my face to strike destructively against the ground. It appears that I tasted the yellow water which flowed from the fountain near the fire and when I did so, I was terribly startled. I took a drop of it in the palm of my hand and swallowed it appreciatively. What do you say it was? *Whiskey*! It was yellow and sharp but it really had the correct taste. In front of me a stream of whiskey was coming from the rock and flowing away, unbought and undrunk. Amazement surged up in my head until it injured me. I went to the well on my knees, to the place where the yellow water was bursting up, and consumed enough to set every bone a-tremble. I looked sharply at the fire while I was near it and it was evident that here was another small fountain of the same spirits but this one, however, was alight and the flames rose and fell accordingly as the stuff was issuing forth.

At any rate, that is how matters stood. If Maeldoon O'Poenassa were dead, it was apparent that he had lived for ages on the nourishment of whiskey from the first well and was protected against cold by the second, quietly spending his life, free from all want, as Sitric O'Sanassa had long ago among the seals.

I looked at him. No stir was made by him, even that of breathing. Fear did not permit me to go to him where he was but I made some rude noises from my position and cast a light stone which hit the bridge of his nose. He did not stir.

- He has nothing to say, said I, half to myself and half aloud.

My heart faltered once more. I heard a sound coming from the corpse which resembled someone speaking from behind a heavy cloak, a sound that was hoarse and drowned and inhuman which took my bodily vigour from me for a little while.

- *And what narrative might give thee pleasure?*[2]

I remained dumb without the opportunity of answering the question. Then I saw the dead person—if he were dead or only soaked with spirits-weariness—endeavouring to settle himself on his stony seat, to shove his hooves in the direction of the fire and to clear his throat for storytelling. The puny voicelet issued from him once more and I almost died with terror:

- *It is unknown wherefore the yellow-haired, small, un-energetic man was named the Captain—he whose place and habitation and steadfast home was a little lime-white house in the corner of the valley. He was wont to spend the year from Hallowe'en until May Day carousing in Scotland and from May Day until Hallowe'en carousing in Ireland. At one time . . .*[3]

On hearing these ghostly words, I do not know whether I was seized by a flood-tide of sickness or terror or of disgust, but finally I laid hold on my courage and, when I became aware once more of the great movement of the universe, I was outside beneath the sharp lashes of the rain with the

bag of gold on my thin bare back and slipping downhill
towards the plain, aided by stream and slope. For a while I
felt I was in the limitless skies, at another time submerged,
for yet another while broken and bruised against the rocks
with sharp and heavy objects falling thickly upon, splitting
my head and my body at yet another time. Doubtless, the way
downhill was frightful and misfortunate when I was returning from the mountain but early in the journey I received
some blow from a pinnacle of rock which deprived me of any
command I had over my senses and down I went as a wisp
without feeling or reason, carried by wind and water.

When I regained consciousness, it was morning and I was
stretched on my back in the soft and most filthy filth which
is nowhere else to be found except in Corkadoragha. All my
skin was ripped and torn like an old suit of clothes but the
bag of gold was still secure in my grasp despite the buffeting
suffered by my hands during the journey. I was still a mile
from the little house which was home and sleeping quarters
for me.

If I was fatigued and exhausted, I was satisfied. I spent
half an hour endeavouring to stand on my feet. When I
succeeded finally, I buried the gold and set off for home
limping. I had the money! I was in possession and had won!
I endeavoured to strike up a little tune but no sound issued
from me. My throat was punctured and, truly, neither my
tongue nor my mouth were in good condition.

When I came to the doorway without a stitch of clothes,
the Old-Grey-Fellow was there and tending his pipe,
pondering at his ease the hard times. I greeted him quietly.
He gazed at me for a while, sharply and silently.

- Upon me soul! said I, I'm ravenous for spuds after
crawling in the sea-water for the good of my health.

The Old-Fellow removed the pipe from his beak.

- There's no understanding the world that's there today at

all, said he, and especially in Corkadoragha. A pig rambled off on us a little while ago and when he returned, he had a worthwhile suit of clothes on him. You went off from us fully-dressed and you're back again as stark-naked as you were the day you were born!

At this stage I was guiding the potatoes from mouth to stomach and he received no reply from me.

E WHO IS threatened throughout his life with misery and is
short of potatoes, does not understand easily what happiness is
nor the management and correct handling of wealth either.
After my journey to Hunger-stack, I lived again for a year
in the old Gaelic manner—wet and hungry by day and by
night and unhealthy, having nothing in the future but
rain, famine and ill-luck. The bag of gold was safely in
the ground and I had not yet taken it to the surface. I
spent many nights in the rushes at the end of the house
scourging my mind, trying to decide what I should do with
the money or what fine and uncommon article I might buy
with it. It was a hard, impossible task. I thought first of
buying foodstuffs but since I had tasted nothing except fish
and potatoes, it was unlikely that the variety of foods consumed by the gentle-folk of Dublin would agree with me
even if I had the opportunity of buying them or even knew
their names! I then bethought me of liquor but I remembered

that few people took to drink in Corkadoragha who were not wafted on death's way after the first bout. I considered buying a hat as a shelter against the rain but decided that no hat existed which would last five minutes undamaged and unrotted by the edge of the weather. The same held good for clothing. The Old-Grey-Fellow possessed a golden watch since the day of the feis but I never understood the utility of that small machine or what point on earth there was to it. I desired neither cup nor household furniture nor pig-platter. I was sunk in poverty, half-dead from hunger and hardship; yet I failed to think of any pleasant useful object that I needed. Certainly, it seemed to me, the rich ones had worry and fret of mind!

I arose one morning when the rain was splashing out of the skies. I was feeble for a time about the house, without interest in anything and not paying any attention to any one thing more than the other. Suddenly I noticed that the floor of the house was red—black-red in places and brown-red elsewhere. I was amazed at this and accosted my mother while she was engaged in pig-feeding activities by the fireside.

- Is it the way, good woman, said I, that the end of the world and the termination of the universe is with us at long last and that there are red showers down on top of us in the dead of the night?

- No and it's not that way, ugly little treasure! said she, but the Old-Grey-Fellow is spouting blood here all the morning.

- I believe that it was out of his nose that this fountain of blood was belching? said I.

- No and it's not that way, little kisser! said she, but deadly unhealable wounds that he has got in his two feet. He had a competition here this morning with Martin O'Bannassa to see who'd lift a big piece of a rock. Poor Martin was beaten, God save the hearers! because he couldn't move the rock. The Old-Fellow was lucky as he always is. He managed to lift the rock as high as his waist and he won whatever stake that they had between them.

- He was always strong! said I.

- But then, because of the amount of the weight, the stone fell from his hands and fell misfortunately on his two feet so that they burst and every bone and bonelet in them was broken, I fear. The ugly fellow was going around the house, shouting for a long time after this work but whatever means of movement he had, it wasn't his feet.

- I never thought, said I, that the Old-Fellow had that much blood.

- If he had, said she, he doesn't have it now!

It happened that this set me meditating on the money that I possessed. If the Old-Fellow had been wearing boots, I thought, less damage might have been done when the stone landed on his hooves. Who knew but that my own feet might be injured and damaged in like manner? What better article might I buy but a pair of boots?

The following day I set out for the place where I had the bag of gold underground. I fell in with Martin O'Bannassa along the road and questioned him about mercantile matters, although I had no experience of them.

- A question for you, Martin, friend, said I. Do you know any words for boots?

- I do indeed, said he. I remember one day being in Derry and eavesdropping in that city. A man went into a shop there and bought boots. I heard clearly the words he spoke to the shopkeeper—*bootsur*. Without a doubt, that is the English for boots—*bootsur*.

- I give you thanks, Martin, said I, and another thanks on top of that one.

I set out. The bag of gold was safe where I had left it. I took out twenty golden pennies and replaced the bag again in the ground. When that task was completed, I went off sturdily for whatever city I might meet as I walked towards the west—Galway or Caherciveen or some other place such as these. There were many houses and shops and people there; business noisily proceeding on every side. I searched the town until I found a boot-shop and I went in cheerfully. A genial portly man was in charge of the shop and when he laid eyes on me, put a hand in his pocket and offered me a red penny.

- Away now, islandman! said he without bitterness in his voice nevertheless.

I received the penny gratefully, put it in my pocket and took out one of my own golden coins.

- And now, said I courteously, *bootsur!*

- *Boots?*

- *Bootsur!*

I do not know whether the fellow was either amazed or did not understand my English, but he stood for a long while gazing at me. He then moved back and fetched many pairs of boots. He gave me my choice. I took the most elegant pair; he took the golden penny and both of us returned our several thanks. I bundled the boots into an old sack which I had and set out on the road home.

Yes! I experienced both fear and shame with regard to the boots. Since the day of the great feis, there were neither boots nor any trace of them to be noticed in Corkadoragha. These elegant bright objects were matters for fun and mockery to the people. I feared that I might become a butt for ridicule in front of the neighbours if I could not educate them previously about the elegance and cultivation connected with boots. I decided to hide the boots and ponder the question at my ease.

After a month I was becoming discontented about these same boots. I possessed them and yet did not. They were in the ground and I did not profit by them when I bought them.

I never had them on my feet and lacked even a minute's experience of wearing them. If I did not acquire some practice with boots secretly and some knowledge of the skill of boot-movement in general, I should never have sufficient boldness to appear in them before the public.

One night (the most nocturnal night I ever knew because of the quantity of rain and the blackness of the black-darkness) I arose from the rushes on the quiet and journeyed out through the countryside noiselessly. I went to the boot-grave and dug them up to the surface with my hands. They were slippery, wet, soft and pliable so that my feet fitted into them without too much difficulty. I tied the laces and went through the countryside, the venomous wind tearing me and the squalls of rain belting the crown of my head abominably. I surmise that I travelled ten miles by the time I reburied the boots. They pleased me greatly in spite of the foot-squeezing, tormenting and foot-hurt I received from them. I was very exhausted when I reached the rushes before daybreak.

It was the time for morning-potatoes when I awoke and hardly on my feet when I noticed that something in life was awry. The Old-Grey-Fellow was away from home (which never happened at potato-time) and the neighbours were standing in small groups, conversing together fearfully and in undertones. Everything looked eerie and the very rain appeared uncommon. My mother was worried and silent.

- Is it the way, loving maiden, said I softly, that the Gaelic misery is at an end now and that the paupers are waiting for the final explosion of the great earth?

- The story is worse than that, I think, said she.

I failed to draw another word from her because of the worried displeasure which had come over her. I moved out. I noticed Martin O'Bannassa out in the field, looking

♣ *I do not know whether the fellow was either amazed or did not understand my English, but he stood for a long while gazing at me. He then moved back and fetched many pairs of boots. He gave me my choice. I took the most elegant pair; he took the golden penny and both of us returned our several thanks. I bundled the boots into an old sack which I had and set out on the road home.*

fearfully at the ground. I moved over until I stood with him and bestowed my blessing most courteously upon him.

- What bad news has come to the village, said I, or is it some new defeat that is in store for the Gaels?

He did not reply for a little while and when he spoke, the hoarseness of terror was in his voice. He placed his lips to my ears.

- Last night, said he, the evil thing was in Corkadoragha.
- The evil thing?
- The Sea-cat! Look!

He pointed his finger towards the ground.

- Look at that spoor, said he, and that spoor! Both of them crossing the country!

I released a small startled sound from me.

- It wasn't cows nor horses nor pigs nor any earthly type that left them, said he quickly, but the Sea-cat from Donegal. May we all be safe! It's a misfortunate, catastrophic, unutterable thing the bad plight and the ill-luck that will come upon us after this day. Of course, 'twould be better for a fellow to jump into the sea and reach eternity. Bad as that place is, the lot that will be ours in Corkadoragha from now on will be infernally insufferable.

I agreed sorrowfully with him and departed. Without a doubt, Martin and the neighbours were referring to my boot-marks. I feared to inform them of the truth because they would have jeered me or set out to slay me.

This wonder lasted for two days, everyone expecting that the heavens would collapse or that the ground crack and the people would be swept away to some lower region. I was relaxed during all this time, free of fear and enjoying the special information which I carried in my heart. Many persons congratulated me on my courage.

On the morning of the third day, I noticed when I arose that we had company in our house. A big tall stranger was standing outside the door, conversing with the Old-Fellow. He wore good navy-blue clothes, bright buttons and huge big boots. I heard him speak in bitter English while the Old-Fellow endeavoured to appease him in Gaelic and broken English. When the stranger observed me at the end of the house, he ceased speaking and leaped through the rushes until he reached me. He was a rough burly fellow and he set my heart trembling with fear. He took a firm grip of my arm.

- Phwat is yer nam? said he.

I nearly swallowed my tongue through sheer fright. When speech returned, I replied to him:

- Jams O'Donnell.

He then let loose a stream of English which overwhelmed me like the nocturnal water. I did not understand a single word. The Old-Fellow approached and spoke to me.

- It was the Sea-cat and no doubt about it, said he, and the first misfortune has arrived. What we have here is a peeler and 'tis yourself that he's looking for.

When I heard this talk a great nervous trembling came upon me. The peeler released another stream of English.

- He's saying, said the Old-Fellow, that some scoundrel murdered a gentleman in Galway lately and that he stole a lot of gold pieces from him. He says that the peelers have evidence that you were buying things with gold a while ago and he says that you're to lay out all you have in your pocket on the table.

The peeler emitted an angry bark. If I failed to understand the words, the roughness of his voice was intelligible indeed. I placed the contents of my pockets on the table, even the nineteen pieces of gold. He glanced at them and then at me. When he had satisfied his eyes, he vomited out other shouts in English and took a firmer hold on me.

- He's saying, said the Old-Fellow, that 'twould be a good thing if you'd go with him.

♣ *We approached timidly and slowly towards one another, filled with fear
and welcome. I noticed that he was trembling, his lips were shaking and
lightning shot from his eyes. I spoke to him in English.*
  - Phwat is yer nam?
He spoke voice-brokenly and aimlessly.
  - Jams O'Donnell! said he.

After hearing this statement, I fear that I lost my senses and that my command over life and limb and person was minimal. I could not distinguish night from bright day nor rain from drought at that moment in the end of the house. Darkness gathered around me and distraction. For a while I recognised nothing around apart from the hold which the peeler had upon me and that we were proceeding together along the road, far away from Corkadoragha, where I had spent my life and where my friends and my kinsfolk had lived since bygone days.

I half-remember being in a big city full of gentlefolk wearing boots; they were speaking sincerely together, going by and climbing into coaches; no rain fell and the weather was not cold. I have a faint memory of being in a noble palace; being a while with a great crowd of peelers who spoke to me and to one another in English; being yet another while in prison. I never understood a single item of all that happened around me nor one word of the conversation nor my interrogation.[1] I remember slightly being in a large ornate hall with others before a gentleman who wore a white wig. Many other elegant people were there, some speaking and others listening. This business continued for three days and I was greatly interested in everything that I saw. When all this was completed, I believe I was imprisoned again.

One morning I was awakened early and ordered to prepare at once to move. This order left me between worry and joy. I was safe and dry and free from hunger while locked up but, nevertheless, I desired to be back once more with my people in Corkadoragha. But to my amazement, it was not towards the town that the peelers took me but towards some place they call a *station*. We were there for a time while I gazed with interest at the great coaches going by pushing big black objects ahead of them which were sniffing and coughing and emitting suffocating smoke. I noticed another pauper who had a Gaelic appearance about him coming into the station with two peelers while he conversed with them in English.

I paid no attention to him until I felt after a while that he was alongside me and addressing me.

- It's clear, said he in Gaelic, that you're in no good situation at present.

- I like this place well enough, said I.

- Do you understand, said he, what you have got from the gentlemen and big bucks of this town?

- I understand nothing, said I.

- You've got twenty-nine years in jail, friend, and you're being brought to that other prison now.

It was a little while before I understood the meaning of this talk. Then I collapsed in a faint on the ground and I should be there still in the same shameful state were it not that a bucket of water was thrown over me.

When I was set on my feet again, I felt light in the head and half-conscious. I observed that certain coaches had come into the station and that people, both gentle-folk and paupers, were coming out of them. I laid my eyes on one man and, without any volition on my part, my gaze remained on him. It was apparent to me that there was something familiar about him. I had never seen him before but he was not a stranger in appearance. He was an old man, bent and broken and as thin as a stem of grass. He wore dirty rags, was barefooted and his two eyes were burning in his withered skull. They stared at me.

We approached timidly and slowly towards one another, filled with fear and welcome. I noticed that he was trembling, his lips were shaking and lightning shot from his eyes. I spoke to him quietly in English.

- Phwat is yer nam?

He spoke voice-brokenly and aimlessly.

- Jams O'Donnell! said he.

Wonder and joy swept over me as flashes of lightning out of the celestial sky. I lost my voice and I nearly lost my senses again.

My father! my own father!! my own little father!!! my kinsman, my progenitor, my friend!!!! We devoured one another with our eyes eagerly and I offered him my hand.

- The name and surname that's on me, said I, is also Jams O'Donnell. You're my father and it's clear that you've come out of the jug.

- My son! said he. My little son!! my little sonny!!!

He took hold of my hand and ate and swallowed me with his eyes. Whatever flood-tide of joy had come over him at that time, I noticed that the ugly fellow had little health; certainly, he had not benefited from the bout of joy which he derived from me at that hour in the station; he had become as white as snow and saliva dripped from the edges of his lips.

- I'm told, said I, that I've earned twenty-nine years in the same jug.

I wished that we had had conversation and that the eerie staring, which was confusing us both, should cease. I saw a softness creep into his eyes and quiet settle over his limbs. He beckoned with his finger.

- Twenty-nine years I've done in the jug, said he, and it's surely an unlovely place.

- Tell my mother, said I, that I'll be back . . .

A strong hand suddenly grasped the back of my rags, rudely sweeping me away. A peeler was assaulting me. I was sent into a running bound by a destructive shove in the small of the back.

- *Kum along blashketman!* said the peeler.

I was cast into a coach and we set out on our journey without delay. Corkadoragha was behind me—perhaps for ever—and I was on my way to the faraway jail. I fell on the floor and wept a headful of tears.

Yes! that was the first time that I laid eyes on my father and that he laid eyes on me; one wee moment at the station and then—separation for ever. Certainly, I suffered Gaelic hardship throughout my life—distress, need, ill-treatment, adversity, calamity, foul play, misery, famine and ill-luck.

I do not think that my like will ever be there again!

NOTES

(D. ... *An Béal Bocht*, Dolmen Press, Dublin, 1964)

Chapter 1

1 *diversions*: Appears in D. as *divarsions* which is explained in a footnote as *scléip* (fun, revelry).

2 *adventures*: In D. appears as *advintures*; explained in foot-note as *eachtraí* (adventures).

3 ... *the end of the house*: This phrase appears again and again in the text; *tóin an tí* in Gaelic (lit. the backside of the house!)

4 ... *a child among the ashes*: Translation of a cliché used continually by Máire (Séamas Ó Grianna) in his novels (ina thachrán ar fud a' ghríosaigh).

5 *explanation*: Myles uses *axplinayshin* in D. and in a foot-note explains: *cúis, bun an scéil* (cause, basis of the story).

6 *animals*: Myles used *béastana* which he explains in a foot-note as *beithidhigh*, cf. *Béarla* 'bastes' (beasts, cf. English 'bastes'!).

7 ... *its like will ever be there again*: This translation of the celebrated phrase used by Tomás Ó Criomhthainn in his *An t-Oileánach* (Dublin, 1927) is one of the ever-recurring

sayings used by Myles in *An Béal Bocht*. Ó Criomhthainn's statement is . . . mar ná beidh ár leithéidí arís ann (because our likes will not be there again).

Chapter 3

1 *grey-wool breeches*: In Gaelic '*brístí de ghlas na gcaorach*', this phrase occurs in books written by writers such as Máire. The wool is undyed. The Gaelic writers generally refer only to the breeches as if the child wore nothing else!

2 *Bonaparte* . . . : In Gaelic this occurs as '*Bonapáirt Mícheálangaló Pheadair Eoghain Shorcha Thomáis Mháire Sheáin Shéamais Dhiarmada* . . .' This is more euphonious than the translation but Gaelic here has the advantage because of the possibility of using genitive cases for each word after the first one.

3 *Jams O'Donnell*: In Máire's novel, *Mo Dhá Róisín*, the author speaks of a pupil hearing himself called by his official name *James Gallagher* on his first schoolday. He had never heard it before! Myles seems to use the name as a generic term for the Gaeltacht man as seen by those outside his boggy rainy ghetto.

4 *sor*: In D. this spelling appears for *sir*. The Gaelic pun is untranslatable—*sor* means *louse* in English!

5 *gramophone*: In D. the word is *gramofón* and in early editions *gramafón* which contain a footnote (omitted in D.) which states: *fónagram*.

6 *Jimmy Tim Pat*: This, of course, should be *Jimmy, son of Tim, son of Pat* but it is left as in Gaelic because this form of nomenclature is quite common in parts of the Limerick, Cork and Kerry countryside still. It is limited, however, to three names unlike the jocular ancestral invocation referred to in note 2 above.

Chapter 4

1 *Father Peter*: This is Father Peter O'Leary (an t-Athair Peadar Ó Laoghaire) the Cork priest whose insistence on the use of ordinary everyday speech in Gaelic literature was such an influential factor in the development of modern writing in the language.

2 *My Friend Drumroosk*: In the original this is: *Mo Chara Droma Rúisc* which may mean either *My Carrick-on-Shannon* or *My Friend D.* as above. The pun is untranslatable.

3 *No liberty without royalty*: This appears as *Ní saoirse go Seoirse—No liberty without George*. To retain the alliterative and syllabic correspondence in translation as in Gaelic, *royalty* has been used.

4 *misfortune . . . misfortune*: The original Gaelic expression *Thit and lug ar an lag orm* means *I became extremely dismayed* while literally it is: *The lug fell on the lag on me!* To retain sense and style, *misfortune* and *misadventure* have been used.

Chapter 5

1 *shadows . . .* : This is commentary on the Gaelic expression *Ar scáth a chéile a mhaireann na daoine* (People live in one another's shadows), meaning *People depend upon one another*.

2 Throughout this chapter in Gaelic snatches of Ulster dialect are used. Except in a few cases, this has not been represented in translation.

3 *Séadna*: This is the title of a famous book by Fr Peter O'Leary (published 1904) which has been the most influential work of his and a book of major importance in modern Gaelic literature.

Chapter 7

1 In Gaelic the saying 'Beidh lá eile ag an bPaorach!' (Power will have another day) is supposed to have been first used by Edmund Power of Dungarvan in the autumn of 1798 as he stood on the gallows, a position which negatived the hope expressed in the saying! In *An Béal Bocht* parodies the expression in 'O'Sanassa will have another day'. By the way, the original saying was often on the lips of Mr Eamon De Valera.

Chapter 8

1 *Maeldoon O'Poenassa*: Note that *Immram Maíle Dúin* (The Voyage of Maeldoon), an ancient Gaelic story of the eighth or ninth century, provided Myles with the name of the gentleman in this chapter who sailed through the Deluge to Hunger-stack.

2 and 3 These portions of the chapter are written in the form of Gaelic used during the period AD 1000–1250.

Chapter 9

1 The assertion by O'Coonassa that he understood nothing of his trial and, later on, of his sentence is reminiscent of very many injustices inflicted on Gaelic speakers in Ireland during the years of British rule. Especially notorious was the hanging of the Joyces in Dublin in the last century after a trial which they never understood and for a crime which they did not commit.